NO DISTANCE TO RUN

No Distance To Run

LEENNA NAIDOO

Tall Fin Publishing

CONTENTS

Excerpt: Situation No Win

CONTENTS DESCRIPTION

Chapter Seven

"Tell me about energy healing. You seem intelligent. How could you possibly believe in it?"

Chapter Eight

I stared at my trusty old Nokia wondering...

Chapter Nine

Jay absentmindedly held the door for me, lost in dark thoughts.

Chapter Ten

The restaurant was cosy, made to look like a farmhouse kitchen.

Chapter Eleven

We reached the mall in the late afternoon.

Chapter Twelve

"Are you going out with him?" Jay was driving us down to Durban again.

Chapter Thirteen

Terry's place was a little daunting at first.

Chapter Fourteen

"I've just read your mind, sweetie. You know you're gonna die, don't you?"

Chapter Fifteen

Three hours later we were still waiting for news of Malcolm.

Chapter Sixteen

I was already moving as fast as I could, the dreadful thought of being stranded on board spurring me on.

Excerpt from *Situation No Win*

About Leenna

More Books By Leenna

NOTE TO READER

This story takes place sometime in the early to mid 2000s, before smartphones and widespread cellphone coverage was the norm in South Africa.

Most of the places are, or were real, and I've written them as I recalled details and impressions from my experiences. Some places, like the Ladysmith Police Station and canteen, I've never been to, and so have used artistic license to fit my story. Forgive me if it ranges too far from reality.

I'd also like to acknowledge my sister and brother without whom I'd never have driven the many roads across the Highveld and beyond, nor taken the bus to Grahamstown.

Many thanks and hugs to all our friends, family, and those kind, hospitable strangers across our varied and beautiful land who made each journey safe and memorable.

And yes, I miss my trusty old Golf!

Leenna Naidoo
November 2022

N.B This story is written in South African English.

~ 1 ~

THE LABYRINTH

I touched my brakes briefly, not bothering to change down a gear on the familiar road. My trusty old CitiGolf took the speed bump like a horse going over an easy hurdle. I kept to third gear knowing the next bump was less than a minute away. Rina had actually turned back to watch the black BMW320i. It had been sitting on our tail hooting irritably for at least the past three minutes. The BMW braked hard but still went over the bump with what must have been an annoying scrape.

Lindi cackled wickedly. "You're evil, darling."

"Don't be silly," I said. "Everyone in Joburg knows all the speed bumps and potholes. And if you don't know the road, you shouldn't be driving so fast."

"Yes. Everyone in Joburg drives too fast!" added Rina, who'd recently moved up from Ladysmith.

"Uh-oh. I can feel a Durbanite Joburg bite coming on...," grinned Lindi, giving us her signature hair pat and wiggle.

I caught Rina's eye in the rear-view mirror. We both shook our heads. I'd been in Joburg for seven years now and didn't consider myself a Durbanite any more. We listened to Björk as I turned left, then right onto William Nicol heading towards Randburg.

"So you're really doing it, Sammi?" asked Lindi.

Rina inched forward on the back-seat.

"*Ja.* It feels like the right thing to do."

"You sure?" asked Rina, "Because my cousin Priya from New-castle went to this astrologer lady in Dundee, and she told her she'd meet the man she'd marry on a cruise. So, Priya used all her saving to go on this cruise and almost died!"

"How? In the swimming pool?" I wondered out loud as Lindi looked at Rina with wide eyes.

"The ship sank."

"The *Achille Lauro?*" went Lindi.

"No, *The Oceanus.* So it just goes to show!" replied Rina, sitting back with satisfaction as we turned into Peter Place and started to move at a more acceptable pace despite the start of the Easter weekend afternoon traffic.

"This isn't the same...," I said lamely, knowing they'd never understand. Rina was only twenty-four, yet already married with a child planned for the next year. Lindi didn't believe in romance and life-long commitment—something her girlfriend found hard to deal with.

"What you need," began Lindi in her Mama-knows-best voice, "is some fun! When was the last time you just went on a fun date?"

I didn't reply, still too mortified to tell them the awful truth.

"Yes," put in Rina, adjusting the *bindi* on her forehead. "When was the last time you *had* a date, never mind a boyfriend?"

I opened my mouth and shrugged, trying to think of something off-hand to say. I was saved the trouble by a taxi suddenly cutting in front of me. I braked heavily and Rina's small purse went flying into the side of Lindi's big, new hair.

* * *

My sister, it seemed, had similar misgivings.

"Look, Sam, you're thirty-three. You've been waiting too long for the 'right man'. Don't you think it's time you opened your mind a bit. There're some genuinely nice guys out there."

I stared at my phone hatefully, half wishing we were back in the days of landlines only—or cellphones without loudspeakers.

She continued, "What about that delivery guy you were talking about?"

"*What!* He's like twenty-three!"

"So?" Easily said if you're married, Aquarian, and a femme-fatale yourself.

"So?" I echoed. "It's not right for me. I need to marry a Taurean born in the year of the Rat 'cos I'm a Cancerian born in the year of the Dragon!"

My sister sighed in exasperation. "You're so stupid sometimes. Just don't get conned, is all I'm saying. I've got to go back underground. I have to inspect a new seam. Love you. Bye. Oh, by the way, are you coming over on Sunday afternoon?"

"Yes, see you then. Love you, too. Bye." I sighed then lugged my suitcase out to the car.

For most of the drive to Magaliesberg, I sang along to my favourite songs which helped keep my mind off the next two days ahead and the fact that I was driving through country roads in the dark— alone. I reached the lodge without incident just after 7 p.m.

Mary, my friend and life-coach, was there to meet me with her famous hug and irrepressible exuberance. Linking her arm through mine, she steered me first to the main farmhouse to point out the dining room and lounges—telling me all the while about the schedule—before leading me down the enchantingly lit path to my door.

"This is a really special time, Sammi. I can just feel it!" she enthused, giving me one last hug before leaving me to settle in.

At 8pm, it was time to go meet the other nine on the course. Introductions were brief. We were left to mingle over a buffet in the dining room of the converted farmhouse. It made for a warm and cosy feel just right for exhaustion to hit despite the strangers and my reason for being there. I thankfully seated myself down by the fire with a plate of snacky things, placing a glass of red wine by my side.

Mary bustled over. "I'm so glad you're here!" she said with a hint of nervousness, squeezing my arm affectionately.

A momentary doubt flitted through my mind. If Mary, the facilitator of our Heart-To-Heart course, was feeling nervous... "It's gonna be great!" I smiled with more assurance than I felt.

Mary smiled back, nodding. "You should mingle," she encouraged, popping a kebab into her mouth.

"I will. I just feel a bit...beat."

"That banshee of a boss been screaming again?"

"*Ja*. We almost missed the deadline for *The Times*. Lost booking materialised."

"What, again? Heads will roll," stated Mary ominously, waving encouragement to a mousey-looking person called Susie or Susan or Sheila.

"Definitely," I remarked absentmindedly as I let my gaze wander over the male occupants of the room. None of them looked like the soulmate I'd envisioned.

Mary started to brief me on the possible matches.

"That's Henry. He's an accountant and a Reiki Master. That's Matthew, a freelance writer and astrologer. Over there is Vusi—owns his own small ad agency. He's a Wiccan. You two have a lot in common. Next to him is Wilhelm, another accountant with big plans to open a retreat near Rustenburg. And last, but not least, we have Malcolm. He's a healer and a vet. You have a lot in common with him, too. He could really help you with your healing development." Mary looked at him thoughtfully. "And he's Taurean."

I looked at Malcolm obediently. His back was to me. It was a nice, well-formed back in a white shirt. His reddish brown hair was neatly cut. Blue jeans and *takkies* completed the look. All in all, a pleasing back.

Mary glanced at me. "Come on, I'll introduce you."

"Um..."

"Come on! Don't be such a chicken or you'll never get anywhere!"

She grabbed my arm, pulling me towards Malcolm and Susie or Susan or whatever-her-name.

The familiar panic set in. I quickly disentangled myself from Mary before we reached the pair. "I'm sorry, Mary. I just need some time to myself. I'm going to go to the labyrinth, then to bed. Okay?"

"Okay." Mary was looking at me with disappointment. "You rest and think about what we talked about. Any of these guys would be a great match for you, but it's up to you to make them see you'd be best for them. Goodnight, sweetie."

She gave me a hug.

"Goodnight, Mary." I scooted out of there as fast as I could.

* * *

I walked down through the trees towards the labyrinth. Three firebrands flickered at the edges of the clearing giving the whole scene a *Survivors Magaliesberg* look. The mountains were faintly drawn in the background, illuminated either by a town or a veld fire—I couldn't tell which.

I stepped softly, not wanting to destroy the almost magical atmosphere, watching my footing on the gravel path to avoid slipping. I'd almost reached the nearest firebrand, allowing me to vaguely make out the dark shape of the tall centre stone, when the shadow of the standing stone struck me as odd. Deformed. Like some nasty shadow creature squatted at its base.

Gripped by a primeval fear, I took a step back. Intent on running to the light and safety of the cottages, I tripped on a treacherous stone. I shrieked as I fell, attempting to skate on the damp grass to retain some balance. At once, a high-powered LED light from the standing stone blinded me.

An angry voice demanded, "What the hell are you doing here?" A male voice; accent indeterminable. Register low. Menacing.

I lost my balance completely, hitting the ground with a thump. Survival instincts taking over, I scrambled up and started to run back to safety. I'd barely taken two steps when I was jerked back painfully by the arm and swung around. The horrid LED light hit me in the eyes. Too terrified to scream, I hit out wildly with my free hand at what I thought would be a face. I jarred a solid arm instead. The torch went flying. He dived for it, his grip loosening on me. *Self Defence 101* coming back to me, I kicked him as hard as I could. As he rolled away gasping in pain, I picked up the torch, taking a second to blind him with it, then raced away, frantically trying to turn the thing off.

I found the switch seconds before I reached the trees. Softly, I darted into the darkness of the copse, carefully stepped off the path and leant against a tree, trying to quieten my breathing. I was absolutely certain he was chasing me. Sure enough, he was.

Seconds later, rapid footfalls announced his approach, slowing as he reached the darkness of the trees. He stopped. I clutched the torch like a club, praying he would pass me by unawares. The seconds crept by as I strained to hear him—appalled that I couldn't hear him at all. Then he was gliding past my tree like a shadowy spirit.

A minute or two stretched by as I stood dithering whether to run to the farmhouse or back to my cottage. The thought of meeting him on the way didn't bear thinking about.

The sound of Mary and a little group of people coming down the path was a godsend. Sagging with relief, I waited for them to reach my tree before stepping out to meet them. Mary screamed. I screamed. Everyone shouted or yelled in surprise—except for Henry who laughed hard enough to scare away any ghosts.

* * *

I woke up the next morning, stiff and tired, amidst crisp cotton sheets, cellphone inches away from my fingers. It took me a moment to remember I was in the cottage. Thoughts of freshly brewed Nescafe proving too tempting, I pulled off the bedclothes. Intent on the little kettle, I stepped off the bed and almost broke my leg when I tripped on the torch. It stopped me dead; all the terror of the night before seeping back.

I'd babbled my story to Mary and the others as soon as everyone had calmed down. We'd all gone down to the labyrinth to search around the standing stone but had found nothing wrong. There was talk of calling the police and nowhere being safe these days. Mary had offered to sleep in my room, but, looking at the others who seemed to be viewing me as some sort of hysterical flake, I'd decided I'd be okay on my own. In fact, standing in that group had made me doubt my own account, with the terror fading like a bad dream. Except it hadn't been a bad dream. That heavy Coleman torch definitely wasn't mine! Whose was it?

I found my toothbrush in distraction. I reflected on my attacker as I'd seen him last—in the bright LED light rolling about in pain. Dark hair, bright beady dark eyes, a strong nose and a wide mouth...Or was he just grimacing in pain?

I finished brushing my teeth then stepped into the shower. He'd been wearing dark jeans, boots, and a dark shirt, underlining his good build. And he'd been strong, I remembered, rubbing my upper arm ruefully where it had already bruised.

I dressed quickly in preparation for breakfast and the course. Dropping a notebook into my bag, I turned to leave. The torch stood staring balefully back at me. I hesitated a second before quickly putting it into my bag and hurrying off to breakfast.

"Any other strange visitations last night?" asked Melanie who, despite claiming to be a psychic whose only life's purpose was to help people, handed out the snidest remarks of anyone I'd ever met.

I blushed, trying to ignore her.

"Well, stress can manifest itself in strange ways," came Vusi to the rescue, his dark face breaking into a huge, cheeky grin. "I remember when I worked at T&T Ads, I got used to experiencing the weirdest things. Like the time I thought the coffee machine was speaking to me in tongues!"

Everyone laughed, starting a recital of their own funny stress experiences. Vusi winked at me. I gave him a grateful smile over the croissants and cold dishes. The course began soon after. I was paired with Malcolm, ostensibly to help each other develop our healing abilities, but actually to see if there was any chemistry.

Three hours later it was obvious Malcolm and I had as much chemistry as neon and argon. I didn't like Malcolm at all, finding his energy rather abrasive.

"Never mind, Sammi," comforted Mary patting my hand as we watched Malcolm hurry off to Susan/Susie/Sheila's side. "I think Henry likes you very much. He's been asking me all about you and been giving you the eye."

I looked at Mary blankly.

"You know, The Eye," demonstrated Mary, assuming the expression of a bug-eyed locust. "I feel you two will have a remarkable future together."

I turned around to find Henry watching me. He smiled, a shy whimsical smile, adjusted his glasses, then strode heron-like out of the room.

* * *

With a two hour break for lunch, rest, and meditation, I grabbed a quick bite with some water before heading off to the labyrinth, safe in the knowledge that on this beautiful, clear day no-one would dare attack me. Not being entirely stupid though, I approached the labyrinth circumspectly.

With only the breeze to disturb the calm, I took a moment to listen and observe the trees around the labyrinth as well as the long grass bordering the entrance. There appeared to be no-one else around. Satisfied I had the place to myself, I took a small rose quartz out of the basket at the entrance and pulled my special wish-stone out of my jeans pocket. I'd leave both at the centre stone with the hope that my wish would come true.

Reverently, I walked the labyrinth, allowing its calming effect to do its thing as it always did for me. It was hot, the breeze making it pleasantly bearable. I reached the centre in a dreamy haze, kneeling down to gently place my two stones in the pile near the base of standing stone. There, I concentrated on my wish to meet my true-love, my husband. That's when I saw it: a little plastic tube, about the size of a cigarette butt, sticking out at the base of the standing stone. It looked oddly menacing, destroying the sanctity of the labyrinth. Feeling almost compelled, I started digging the object out with my fingernails, certain it would explain why I'd been attacked the previous night.

"Hey, what are you doing?" I jumped at Henry's voice. There had been no hint of his approach.

"You gave me a fright!" I panted, standing up covered in dust and perspiration. That tube was just about out but it was putting up a hard fight.

"Sorry. Did you lose something? Can I help?" Henry's stride cut across the lines of stones, his face lit with a helpful smile.

"Um, no. I was just making a wish."

"Oh," said Henry, stopping just as he reached the centre. "I see."

That smile again, only taking on a false quality. I leant backed against the stone, my body blocking the plastic tube, and slid down to a kneeling position in the stone's shade. Brushing back wet hair off my forehead, I smiled just as falsely wishing he would go away.

He knelt down too. "So..."

He was quite cute, but... "Look, Henry," I began, wanting to get it over with quickly. "I desperately need some time to myself. Do you mind?"

He stared at me a moment. "Um, *ja*. Sure. I'll just...," He got up and began to back off. "Um...See you later?"

"Definitely." I smiled sincerely, suddenly liking him more. I watched him stride off towards the trees, my hidden fingers worrying the tube out of the dusty ground.

A couple of minutes later I had it nestled in my hand. The tube was about two centimetres long, all black with a little seam along its width. A little pressure on the seam popped it open. Inside was a single piece of tightly rolled paper with a stream of printed numbers. A shadow fell across me. "Henry...," I began, already instinctively crumpling the piece of paper into my hand whilst turning to look up. It wasn't Henry. It was my attacker from the previous night. I rose slowly as we eyed each other warily, with him standing no more than a metre or so from me.

He was remarkably handsome in daylight. The dark hair was dark brown; the bright beady eyes were still bright but a light, pure green—not beady at all. His mouth was full, not too wide or small. So he had been grimacing...*Oops!* He wasn't as slim as I'd thought him to be, but broader, lending his appearance more menace in daylight with his arms folded, his legs spread.

His hand extended in expectation for the plastic tube. I complied, holding out the tube.

"Who's Henry?" he rumbled.

"What?" My brain struggled to process his question.

"Who's Henry?"

Help had arrived. I pointed. "Him!"

Henry was running down to the labyrinth, drawing something from his pocket. Good old Henry was calling the police. Mr Menace didn't turn around. He just grabbed my arm again, constantly jerking me off balance, preventing me from running away or attempting to kick him.

"Henry!" I screamed.

Mr Menace turned to face him just as Henry arrived, gun in hand. I stood open mouthed. *Henry with a gun!*

"Hand it over," demanded Henry, not sounding very nice at all.

"But..," I whinged. *Wasn't Henry supposed to save me?*

Mr Menacing stood very still. Silent.

"Hand it over, Sammi. I know you've got it. I don't want to have to shoot you too."

Henry looked way too comfortable with that gun.

"Give it to him." Mr Menace's voice was softly compelling. I held out the black tube once again.

"Throw it," instructed Henry, obviously not keen on stepping any closer to the simmering Menace.

I threw the light tube. It landed in a tuft of dried grass closer to Mr Menace than to Henry.

"Don't move." Henry's voice was cold as he stepped forward.

Keeping the gun trained on us, he knelt down, groping for the black tube.

I could not believe Henry was going to shoot us. He'd already indicated he was going to shoot Mr Menace. There was no reason to think he wouldn't shoot me, too. This was *not* how my life was supposed to end!

A few long moments went by as I waited for my life to flash before my eyes. Instead, I just thought of all the things I'd never get to do.

Henry shifted, glancing down to search for the tube which must have rolled away. It's usually at this point in movies and books that the hero charges the gun-wielder, wrestles it out of the gunman's grip and wins the day. Mr Menace must have watched the same movies as me. He moved abruptly, kicking out at Henry's face, fist hammering down. Henry, somehow anticipating this, moved back and shot him.

My scream seemed disembodied as Mr Menace came toppling down on me. Futilely, I tried to catch him, only to be borne to the ground with him, my hand and body turned to the right as I ended up cradling his torso, still screaming. Henry's triumphant eyes met mine as he stepped forward. He shot Mr Menace again. The bullet jerked his body momentarily off me then slammed me painfully into the ground again, leaving me with no breath.

I passed out.

* * *

My side was burning, pulling me back to consciousness.

A man was crying over sharp, concerned voices. "I could have stopped them! I should have stopped them. If only I...," he sobbed hysterically. It was Henry.

Melanie was comforting him. "There's nothing you could have done. They had guns, lovey. *Toe nou, kom.*"

Henry wasn't going anywhere. "No, no! Maybe I can still help! Maybe she's still alive!" Which was how Henry got to see Vusi and Mary gently roll Mr Menace off me.

I groaned involuntarily. Instantly, Mary and Vusi were attending to me, checking the extent of the wound.

"Let me see!" Henry was trying to push past, but Vusi shoved him gently away into Matthew and Wilhelm's waiting arms. They led him away despite his protests.

"Henry did it!" I tried to say.

"Yes, Henry's fine, sweetie. Don't worry about him," reassured Mary, holding a piece of her torn skirt to my wound.

"Guy...," I tried again.

"He's...not good, sweetie. Malcolm's doing his best."

I passed out again, only to be awakened by new voices. The paramedics and police were quick and efficient. They were working on Mr Menace when I turned my head to him. His green eyes bore into mine. "Gerrie..." I thought I heard him say just before they carried him away on a stretcher. I tried to think. He was attempting to give me a message, surely. But what did it mean? It was no good. I fell into a numbing daze as they lifted me and began carrying me towards the farmhouse.

"She's okay. It's just a flesh wound," someone said.

"Thank God!" I heard Mary say, hurrying alongside.

I was taken to my cottage for treatment. Mary stayed with me the whole time, holding my hand as I drifted in and out of consciousness; partly from the pain, partly from the painkillers. I remembered insisting Henry be kept away from me. Fortunately, Mary listened. No-one else was allowed in with us, except Vusi who spoke quietly with Mary sitting in the window-seat. Their presence was comforting. Eventually, I relaxed into sleep.

~ 2 ~

CAMERA OBSCURA

I awoke in the late afternoon. The soft glow from the window showed Mary and Vusi still sitting on the window-seat talking in low voices. They hurried over when they saw me stir.

"Sammi, how do you feel?" Mary was all concern.

"Thirsty," I croaked. Vusi held my head as Mary fed me some water.

"The Inspector wants to talk to you," Mary began. "I told him you were still unconscious. They need to know what happened."

"Henry shot us."

In the silence, Vusi and Mary exchanged looks." Are you sure, sweetie?" asked Mary gently. "You're in shock and a little confused."

"Henry shot him and me. I was there!" I said more strongly, feeling anger for the first time—along with a great deal more pain. I winced.

Vusi squeezed my hand in sympathy, saying, "I believe you, Sammi. Henry's a fake. I know, I've worked with more than a few."

Mary looked stunned. "But I checked his credentials before I allowed him on the course. Just as I do with everyone!"

"Oh, really?" drawled Vusi, unexpectedly teasing. "And what did you find out about me?" She actually blushed. He was suddenly serious again. "You'll have to tell the police everything, Sammi."

"Yes," added Mary. "Especially with Henry trying to blame everything on two young farmhands. But the police will only be back in the morning."

"And Henry will be back before then." Vusi's tone was dark.

I was immediately more alert. "Where's Henry now?"

"He went to the hospital to see to that guy."

I had almost forgotten about Mr Menace. "Is he...?"

"He's in ICU. They've notified his family. Someone's with him."

I tried to get up, seized by a sudden dread. "Henry will try to kill him again. I have to tell the police!"

But Vusi and Mary were pushing me back, with Vusi saying, "Easy there. I think Inspector Govender is at the hospital. I'll call. You can tell him then."

I settled back as Vusi dialled. Mary fed me more water. Vusi's call was connected. He asked for the Inspector and got a squeaking response. Then he enquired about Mr Menace and Henry. He cut the call sooner than expected, looking grim.

"I couldn't get the Inspector. The guy just died about twenty minutes ago. And Henry left the hospital more than fifteen minutes ago without getting to see him."

Mary looked as shocked as I felt. "I can't be here!" I staggered to my feet woozily, grabbed Mary's shoulder to steady myself and waited for the spinning to stop. "I have to go before he comes back."

"But." Vusi had put his strong arm around me, trying to steer me back to bed. "We're all here now. Malcolm, Matthew, Sheila, Melanie...He can't shoot all of us!"

"He doesn't have to." He tried to stare me down. "Henry shot that guy twice without hesitation. Do you want anyone else here to get hurt?"

His gaze dropped.

"You can't drive in that condition." Mary was all practicalities now. "I'll drive you to the police station."

"We'll all go. Safety in numbers," decided Vusi.

I nodded, the room still reeling around me. Mary helped me gather my stuff. We left soon after.

Vusi lifted me into the back of the Tucson as Mary climbed into the front passenger seat. She pulled a blanket over me. I lay in the back as snug as I'd ever be.

Vusi drove well, going down the country track with cautious—slowing timeously for the dips so I wouldn't be jarred. Just before the main road, an oncoming car caused us to slow even more. Vusi went left to crawl by. The car stopped as it drew level with Vusi's window. Everyone tensed. Vusi wound down his window a little.

"Hi, Henry," he said easily.

"Hi. Is Sammi okay? Is she still at the farm?"

"Last I saw her," replied Vusi, glibly. "It's a bad business."

"Yes," agreed Henry then seemed to register Mary. "Mary," he greeted.

She smiled tensely in reply.

"Where are you guys going?" Henry's voice was casual. "It's late and the roads here aren't that safe, you know." He laughed.

Vusi joined him. "*Ja* man, we know. But the doc left a prescription for Sammi. The hospital's got it ready. We won't be long."

"Right. See you later then," said Henry.

"Later," agreed Vusi, winding up his window, and rolling us past Henry.

"Vusi Shabalala, you lie too easily," observed Mary with relief.

Vusi just grinned as I tried to relax my clenched muscles.

* * *

Inspector Govender was very sympathetic, but not very helpful. He took my statement, not asking many questions, merely sitting there with his foot tapping incessantly. "Just tell me what happened," he had said. So I had. First, I mentioned the previous night of my scare, then the day's events. I didn't think I 'd left anything out. Every now and again, when it seemed I was slowing down, he'd go, "Um...,"or "Er..." which served to prompt me on.

Eventually, when I'd finally wound down and it was apparent I'd nothing more to add, the Inspector said, "Unfortunately, at this point, it's your word against his. We haven't found the gun."

"But—"

"And Mr Wilkins has no gun registered to him. With him having been nowhere near the victim in hospital...You see our problem?"

I did indeed.

"We can't arrest Wilkins without any evidence or a confession."

"And, if he tries to kill me again? Can't you put me into protective custody or something?"

He shook his head. "Look, I'm really sorry, but my arms are tied. Here's my number. Call me any time of the day or night. If you remember anything else or find any evidence."

I remembered then about the little slip of paper in my jeans pocket. I took the Inspector's number, tucking it into the same pocket. That little slip of paper with those numbers didn't prove anything. I could have printed it myself.

The Inspector held the door for me, revealing an anxious Mary and Vusi.

"I'm sorry," stated the Inspector again. "My advice is that you take a holiday for a week or two. Either way, things should be sorted out by then." He shook our hands in turn then walked tiredly back into his office.

Vusi and Mary looked at me. I looked back, a forgotten wave of exhaustion washing over me.

"Come on. Let's get out of here," gestured Vusi. Mary took my arm offering support once more.

* * *

Vusi started the engine. "Where to?"

In silence we sat contemplating.

"She can't come back to the lodge," Mary finally admitted. "We could take you to your sister's...?" She'd turned around to look enquiringly at me.

I thought as best I could. "No, he might find me there too easily."

"Your parents?" suggested Vusi.

"No, same reason."

"You could stay at my place," offered Mary.

I smiled wanly, shaking my head. "I can't let him hurt anyone else if I can help it."

Vusi shook his head in frustration. "It's just not right, man! I'd offer you my place, but it's under renovation. Look, maybe the Inspector's right. A holiday is the answer. Go to the Cape, or the Kruger, or on a cruise or something. Away, you know, from all the things you do and places you usually go."

"I think so, too," agreed Mary. "Can you afford a few days off, sweetie? Take leave and disappear. I can lend you a couple of thousand."

"And I," offered Vusi just as quickly.

They both knew I didn't earn very well and wouldn't have been able to save much after paying for my rent, car and living expenses. Johannesburg was not a place that allowed you to save. I sighed. There went my meagre savings towards that once-in-a-lifetime-trip to Scotland. "I have some money in a savings account. I could go some place for a few days."

"Great! Airport or bus station?" asked Vusi with relief.

I thought a moment. "Bus station."

"Bus station it is!" Vusi got us on our way.

A few minutes passed by as we all thought our own thoughts.

Mary turned around to face me again, "Any ideas on where you'll go?"

I'd been thinking hard about that. "I have a friend staying in Grahamstown. He's always asking me over. And we haven't seen each other for a long time."

"Jay?"

I nodded. "Let me give him a call." I dialled, and was surprised when he picked up almost immediately. "Hi! Jay?"

"Hi, Gorgeous. Long time no squeak."

"*Ja*, I know," I apologised, already feeling a bit better at the sound of his voice. "And it's such short notice, but I was wondering if I could come over to visit you this weekend?"

"What? This weekend! You mean like tomorrow?"

My heart started to sink. It *was* the Easter weekend. It had been stupid of me to even think... Mary was crossing her fingers with her eyes closed, praying for me. "Um, *ja*. If you're free...If not, that's fine. I'll catch you another time..." My voice sounded deceptively bright and cheerful in contrast to my heavy heart.

"Oh, no. I'm all on my lonesome here," came back Jay's easy voice. "Everyone's gone except me and a few cultures. I'd love to have you here. So much more fun than petri dishes."

Coming from Jay, that was a major compliment.

"Great!" I was beaming. "I'll just take the next bus to Grahamstown and text you when we get there."

'Cool! Can't wait to see you," and he cut the call.

Mary and Vusi were both grinning, obviously relieved. All that was needed was the bus ticket, and I only just made it onto the 18h45 to Grahamstown.

"Remember to call!" yelled Mary, standing next to Vusi as the Greyhound jerked and rolled away, heading for Vanderbiljpark.

I smiled and waved, then settled myself in for a sleep.

* * *

I couldn't get comfortable on the bus despite the solicitous hostess's attentions. I dozed listlessly through the movies. Vaguely, I remembered stumbling outside at a stop for the Ladies and some hot-choc. Most of the night journey seemed like a drive through limbo.

I got a fright when we stopped at about 3 a.m., seemingly in the middle of nowhere.

I jerked up, my side protesting as I squinted fearfully around me, certain Henry had already found me before I'd even begun to run. It was only the change of drivers. I watched as our previous driver waved to his colleagues, then thankfully headed in the direction of the Total garage, to disappear into the shadows. Then, we were off again, our new driver's broad Platteland accent joking with the new hostess. I drifted off again.

The day dawned bright and clear with yet more tea and biscuits. In a *dwaal*, I turned to watch the Griquas slide by. At King William's Town, I roused myself sufficiently to text Jay on our progress, then went back into my comforting state.

* * *

That late morning, Jay was waiting for me when the bus stopped on one of the main streets. I descended the steps and went to retrieve my bag as he walked over from his old Pajero—the same one he'd had since Tech. He was beaming as he came in for a hug.

"Hey, Gorgeous!"

I smiled wanly, hugging him gingerly back. "Hey you!" I winced, my side hurting.

At once, he pulled back to scan my face, concerned. "What's wrong?"

Trying not to cry, I took a deep, shaky breath as the bus pulled away.

"Sammi?" His face was now worried, but as kind as ever.

And there, in Grahamstown's main street, I allowed myself to cry and be held by one of my oldest friends.

* * *

"He did what?" Jay had gotten me back to his little town-house, plying me with toast and black Earl Grey.

Feeling drained, I played listlessly with the mug handle, but I felt lot better now I was able to tell my story again—making more sense of it. "Henry just shot the guy. Then he shot him again. He came right up to stand over us, looking into my eyes. I know he meant that second bullet to kill us both."

"Typical accountant," was Jay's dark comment.

I glanced sharply up at him. He didn't look like the funny, easy-going Jay I knew.

His expression was coldly furious. "I'd like to meet that accountant of yours."

I thought of the only time I'd seen Jay angry. I almost wished he would run into Henry. But Henry had a gun. So I said instead, "Don't be silly!"

Jay's smile was crooked. I was always the level-headed one talking him out of silly or downright dangerous things. And here we were, again...

"You can stay for as long as you need. You know that."

I nodded. "Thanks."

He hugged my shoulders. "You look beat. I've got the bed ready. Go have a nap."

I was in total agreement. Falling gently into bed in the little spare/storage room, I drifted quickly to sleep to the sound of Jay singing as badly as ever.

The sun was westering when I woke up to a quiet house. Wondering where Jay had gone, I struggled up stiffly, still feeling a bit dizzy and grateful at how lucky I was to have such a good friend. We'd been through such a lot together. Everyone had been certain we'd have eventually married each other, but there'd never been any romantic chemistry between us. And both of us had agreed that chemistry was all important.

A barely decipherable note revealed Jay had gone to check on his cultures and would be back for supper. I rummaged in the cupboards, feeling a bit peckish. Some biscuits, a cup of tea, and the TV remote got me comfortably settled until I heard my cellphone ringing. At first, I thought it was the TV, then realised it was mine. I staggered off to find the thing. It proved to be hiding in my jacket pocket. As usual, the thing promptly stopped ringing as soon as my fingers touched the casing.

Five missed calls from my sister and two from Mum and Dad. Guiltily, I called them back, trying to make the calls as short as possible, assuring them I was alright, but needed to be away from them just then. Mum and Dad were worried but admitted I should do what I thought best. Typically, Dad was reassured when I told him I was staying at Jay's. I promised to keep them updated as much as I could, and warned them about Henry calling them if he found out their number. My sister had more distressing news when I told her about the change of plans—my not going to Harties.

"But your friend Henry is here! I like him. He's really nice and cute...He's out by the pool with Steve. Wait, I'll put him on."

My blood ran cold. "No!"

"But!"

Jay walked in with a Wimpy bag. Quietly, he went about, his attention pricked. I'd thought fast. My sister couldn't act to save her life.

"I can't talk to him. It's...complicated. Tell him I wouldn't be coming to Harties. That I had to go help a friend in...Dullstroom. Better yet, Nelspruit. Tell him I'm in Nelspruit and not expected back for a while."

My sister gave her long suffering sigh. "I don't think playing hard to get is going to work on a nice guy like Henry. He doesn't look the type who likes playing games."

"Look, I'll explain things some other time. Just tell him I'm in Nelspruit, okay?

"Okay," she agreed with reluctance. "But I think you're making a huge mistake."

Jay raised an enquiring eyebrow as I cut the call.

"Henry's at my sister's."

He did a brief impersonation of a rabbit caught in headlights, then looked thoughtful pulling out a nice bottle of Shiraz. He gestured to the bottle. I shook my head regretfully—antibiotics.

Putting the kettle on instead, he said, "That was fast."

"Yes."

"How do you think he found her?"

"Mary?" I thought out aloud, wearily. I remembered with a jolt I'd forgotten to call her. I dialled quickly.

"Thank God! Did you get to Jay's okay?"

I reassured her, then told her about Henry visiting my sister.

"Oh God! I told him all about you when he asked—before I knew...Where you work, where you're from. About you being the middle child...I'm so sorry, sweetie."

I held my head. "It's not your fault. You weren't to know. I'll call you sometime, okay?" I put my phone down on the table.

"Does she know where I live?"

I nodded. "She knows you live in Grahamstown. But she couldn't have had the time to have such an in-depth discussion about me with Henry."

"No," admitted Jay. "But your sister could have."

"Oh God!" This was getting from bad to worse! I'd thought Grahamstown would be the safest place. "I'm sorry. I should have stayed away from here, too."

Jay grinned, handing me a burger. "Are you kidding! This is just the kind of excitement I was wishing for this Easter. Do you know how bored I've been?" He took a big bite from the first of his two burgers.

I smiled, taking a smaller bite of my own burger. It was good. I hadn't had one in a while. I remembered then. "I have to go to the bank tomorrow. I need to get some funds from my savings."

"No prob. The bank here might open. If not, we'll go to East London."

* * *

The next morning was deliciously bright and sunny as we walked to the bank. The service was miraculously good. Feeling better now that I had more funds available, and with the cheerful look of the town, I let Jay talk me into visiting the Camera Obscura museum that afternoon. First I had a nap, followed by a leisurely lunch at an outdoor café not far from his townhouse.

Along the way, we strolled over to a couple of bookstores where he was greeted like an old friend. It had turned into a beautifully warm afternoon. I let myself be transported by the history and the museum, forgetting about my own predicament for a couple of hours. We went up to the Obscura with the last tour of the day. The guide pulled a few ropes, adjusting the lenses and opening the aperture. A startlingly clear view of the far hillside appeared, helped by the brilliant sunlight. It was fascinating. The guide was good, giving us a historical tour of the various landmarks with some hilarious comments disguising great insight. He zoomed in, as a finale, on the town square. My heart skipped a beat for a couple of seconds. I was certain amongst the milling throng of people, I'd seen the ghost of Mr Menace clear as day.

"Don't be silly," scoffed Jay leading me carefully down the narrow stairs from the tower. "There's no way that a ghost—if you believe in such things—could travel over all this way to haunt you. They are supposed to stick to the place they died."

"Yes, but..."

"But what? You're tired. And, maybe still in some kind of shock. Let's get you home."

We stopped by the Spar for some supplies on the way back to the townhouse.

An Audi A3 was parked in Jay's visitor's bay—silver with tinted windows. I couldn't see in. A nasty feeling crept over me.

"Jay."

"Hmm..." He glanced up from gathering the packets, found me staring at the A3, and read my thoughts effortlessly. "You said he drove a BMW X3, didn't you?"

"Yes."

"And that A3's not a rental. So it can't be him...unless he's clairvoyant!"

I shivered. That thought hadn't occurred to me yet. Even though Jay had meant it as a joke, I'd heard a few stories, as well as having had a few weird experiences myself, to know that such things were possible.

"Come on," chided Jay, opening the door whilst balancing the groceries against his long legs. He went inside. I looked around fearfully before following him, locking the door behind us. Jay came up to hug me. I couldn't help but start sniffling into his shoulder.

"It's going to be alright," he soothed. "I wouldn't let anyone hurt you, okay?"

I nodded, but cried anyway. Some things were difficult to believe.

~ 3 ~

WINBURG

"It's a nap for you and some culture for me!" Jay had said as he let himself out, on the way to the lab.

Smiling, I'd taken his advice and tried to nap, but was too jumpy. I wished desperately for sleep, only to have it prove more and more evasive. Every little sound made me tense up, more alert than ever. Eventually, I heard the front door open. Relieved, I woke up and walked to the kitchen. "Jay?"

The man closing the door wasn't Jay. He was a lot heavier in build. He turned around to lean against the door. I gasped at the sight of his face, stepping back in alarm into the wall. It was Mr Menace. And he most certainly was not a ghost! We stood for a few moments staring at each other, not moving.

His voice was just as I had remembered it—quietly chilling. "We have a lot to talk about, don't we, Samantha?"

"My friend will be back any second," I croaked, trying not to show my trembling.

He narrowed his eyes. "Then we'd better talk fast." He indicated the kitchen chair.

I glanced from it to him, in fear.

"Okay," he said, pulling out the far chair then sat himself down, never taking his eyes off mine.

I cringed closer to the wall. He was giving off seriously unfriendly vibes. Extremely hostile was closer to the truth.

He echoed himself from the night before. "Who's Henry?"

I didn't answer, still trying desperately to think.

Irritated, he leant forward, elbows on the table. "Who's Henry?"

I stepped back instinctively, putting my hand on the spare room door-frame.

"I won't ask you again," he threatened.

"I don't know!" I screamed, spinning around to haul myself through the doorway, and slam the door shut. He hit it just as I turned the lock. I screamed again as his next assault on the door revealed just how flimsy a barrier it was.

Running to the large aluminium windows, I squeezed my clumsy way out, silently thanking Jay for not having put in burglar-guards. Falling into the courtyard, I screamed again as loudly as I could. Behind me, the bedroom door crashed open. Not stopping to think, I bolted through the neighbour's garden and around the corner of their garage. No-one came out to see what the noise was about. I heard Mr Menace run around Jay's house, stopping at the window. As noiselessly as I could, I climbed onto some garbage trolley bins then onto the roof of the garage, my side protesting with every stretch. Easing myself flat on the rough tiles, I could only pray.

He came round the side of the garage to the trolley bins. There he stopped again.

I held my breath for a long moment. Then he was off again, leaving me sweating in the last of the baking afternoon sun and rapidly developing a headache. I didn't move until I heard the slam of the car door followed by its rapid acceleration as he sped away, no doubt figuring I'd gotten onto the main road and was running into town. With awkward movements, I eased myself off the roof onto the garbage trolley bin. It began to wobble and shift. I half jumped, half slid onto the ground, tearing my wound open. Bleeding and swearing in a most unladylike way, I dragged out my cellphone and called Jay.

* * *

He found me curled into the darkest corner of his house, which happened to be in his bedroom. He'd left his curtains drawn. Jay knelt down reaching for my hands.

"There's a bloody hand-print in the bathroom. Is it yours?"

I nodded. I'd thought I'd cleaned up properly after changing my shirt and attending to my side the best I could.

"What happened?" Gently, he tried pulling me up, but I resisted.

"He's no ghost! He was here!"

"The Audi A3?"

"I think so."

Jay nodded then went away. I heard the bathroom tap running. He came back, drying his hands on a towel, looking grim. "How could he have found you? Who is he anyway?"

I shrugged, those very questions having worn a groove in my head the over last twenty minutes.

"What do you want to do?"

"I don't know!" I tried to suppress my tears, the despair welling up further.

"I have to get to Maritzburg by Wednesday. Why don't you come with me?"

I looked at Jay gratefully. "I'd love to."

"Great. Then we'll get started tomorrow morning. Take the scenic route. I'd like to go to Clarens again. See the Golden Gate..."

I knew Jay was trying to distract me. I smiled briefly in appreciation.

The doorbell rang. I tightened into a ball again. Jay shot me a reassuring smile on his way to get the door. I strained to hear. Mr Menace's voice carried easily, unmistakable.

"I'm Inspector Grierson, here to see Samantha Gonzales."

"She's not here," lied Jay.

"I saw her here not an hour ago." Mr Menace 's voice was returning to the Polar regions.

Jay's voice matched the inspector's with quiet obstinacy. "She's not here. And she was hurt last I saw her. Do you know anything about that?"

In the replying quiet, I could imagine Jay squaring off with the other's growing aggressiveness.

"I'd like to check the premises."

"Do you have a warrant?"

Another loaded silence. I was clenching my fists so hard, my hands hurt.

Then, "Interpol?" remarked Jay in surprise. He recovered quickly. "An ID card's not a warrant. Besides, it looks like you printed it off the Internet."

There was a sharp intake of breath, quickly followed by a threat. "Let me in or I'll make sure you're in great trouble in more countries than you've ever visited."

"No," stated Jay calmly, and shut the door. I heard his cellphone dialling. "Yes. There's a man at my front door threatening me..."

Jay had called the local police! I strained again to hear if the A3 had driven off. From the sounds in the kitchen, it seemed Jay was making a cup of tea. He didn't come into the room. I stayed put, realising Menace Grierson was probably still lurking about. We waited for what seemed a long time.

Eventually, I heard a car pull up abruptly.

"Excuse me, sir. But we have a complaint...." came faintly through the window.

* * *

"Interpol!" snickered Jay, driving us through the sunset to East London. "Trust you to do things differently."

I didn't find it funny. Grierson had driven off accompanied by the local police. Jay had suggested I fly out of East London to spend the night in Kimberley, from where he'd fetch me to continue on to Pietermaritzburg.

"Kimberley! But, it's in the opposite direction! That's not on the way."

"It is now!" he'd said with a grin. Less than half an hour later, we were off, with Jay roaring down the country roads and making light of everything again.

"Maybe," he suggested, "You should actually talk to Grierson. Get him off your case."

"Do you really think he is a legitimate law officer?"

"It would explain how he found you so quickly."

"Then why would he wait to question to me alone, hunting me down like that? And he threatened you!"

"Okay. So that's not the way a responsible, nice policeman behaves, but he was shot. Or maybe it was his brother?"

"His twin brother?" I was being sarcastic.

"Exactly. It's more probable than a ghost of the man who was shot...Or that the hospital lied about his death."

"So which one would be the evil twin?"

Jay laughed. I shifted, trying a new position in the shaky Pajero, watching the scenery slide by. He turned up the music to sing along to Blur.

* * *

Jay watched me go through check-in early, then left, needing to get a good night's rest before setting of at 4am the next morning. He'd already booked me into a little hotel in Kimberley where he'd stayed a couple of times before.

"You'll like it. It's very retro!" he'd promised with a grin.

The SAA Express flight was comfortable despite the loud noise of the twin-turbines on the small craft. I enjoyed it, thinking it quite a romantic way to fly. We landed at night in Kimberley. Not having any luggage except my small backpack, I jumped into the first shuttle into town. The driver kindly offered to drop me off at the hotel saying, "You look tired, *meisie*." I accepted gratefully.

Half an hour later, I stood in front of the hotel thinking, *Retro, indeed!* It was an old Forties-style building. Inside proved not much had changed since: neat, well maintained and, with its opulent old furniture, extremely charming.

The receptionist, Marika, turned out to be the owner. She welcomed me warmly, told me the breakfast times and offered her help. "Anything you need, you just ask, okay?"

A bellhop, with one of those pillbox hats and matching smartly piped uniforms, ceremoniously carried my wildly out-of-place backpack up a flight of stairs and into my room. It was the Green Room. The walls a light green, the curtains a dark hunters-green in heavy velvet, matching the carpet. A luxurious striped white and light green duvet covered the soft bed. Green was my favourite colour. I smiled feeling safe again, wondering if Jay had requested this room especially for me. That would be just like him.

After a good breakfast the next morning, I checked out of my room. "Would you mind if I waited here for a few hours? My friend will be arriving to fetch me, but might only be here by midday."

"Sure. No problem. You can just wait in our lounge over there. And if you'd like any tea or coffee, you just let us know, okay?" said Marika, with a sincere smile and hospitality.

"Great." I smiled back, and lugged my backpack over to the lounge indicated.

I found an old M.M Kaye book in the small library to while away the time. A few teas, a wonderful piece of milktart, and a few hours later saw Jay ambling into the reception area. He spoke briefly to Marika, joking, before heading over to the lounge. I was returning the book to its shelf when he walked in. He stopped for a moment, assessing me.

"Hi, Gorgeous. You're looking much better." He grinned.

I smiled, returning his gentle hug. He took my bag. We said goodbye to Marika.

"You must come again, hey."

After assuring her we would, we set off for Clarens via Winburg.

"Did you have any more trouble with Grierson?" It was the only thing besides the throb of my side that had bothered me since leaving Grahamstown.

"He was waiting for me when I got back home," replied Jay, all tranquilly.

I turned in alarm, searching Jay's face, half expecting to see some horrible bruise I might have somehow missed earlier.

He smiled reassurance. "It's okay. He brought a warrant and searched my place."

"Oh no!"

"He found your other bag. Demanded to know where you were and where I'd been. I told him I hadn't seen you since the afternoon and that I'd been to Kendall-on-the-Sea...There's this place that does the best burger, chips, and bunny chow right on the beach."

"Did he believe you?"

"No. Untrusting soul, our Mr Grierson. Made more threats and left shortly after I laughed at him. His Audi was still outside this morning when I left."

"Did he see you?"

"No." Jay's grin was huge. "I rolled the Paj down the drive—only starting it on the road. Don't think he's gonna be too pleased with me."

I shivered, an image of an angry Grierson in my mind's eye. "Jay, be careful. He's a very dangerous man!"

"Mm...," was his unconcerned response, followed by, "Look! Ostrich farm!" He slowed down to let a bird run alongside the fence as we drove by.

"I thought you only see them in Oudtshoorn!" I hadn't seen one in years—not since I was twelve and my family did the whole Durban to Cape Town trip that December.

Jay explained. "There are farms all over now. Ostrich meat is still a big health rage. Croc meat's becoming more popular, too. They're both very tasty."

"Hmm hmm. Healthy they may be, but I can't imagine eating them. I prefer my meat less prehistoric!"

* * *

The road went on ceaselessly, winding up and down hills, opening large vistas of veld only to hide them almost as quickly. The Pajero was dependable, if a little rattly. Then again, it had always been so. I was humming along to U2 when we pulled into a Total Rest-stop in the middle of nowhere. We got out for a stretch. I favoured my hurt side.

"See you in there," Jay indicated the shop and take-away.

I nodded, looking around as he disappeared into the mens room. A tour bus was entering the forecourt. Sighing, I went into the Ladies, not wanting to be caught in the wait when the bus discharged its occupants.

I smiled at one of the ladies in line as I washed my hands.

"It's a beautiful country, yes?" she remarked in a German-sounding accent.

"Yes, it is," I agreed.

"You are English?"

"No," I laughed. "I'm from Durban."

She nodded. "It is by the sea?" It was my turn to nod. "It is very beautiful, too, but we cannot go there this time. We will go next time."

"Yes. You should visit—in August or November, but not February," I suggested. "The weather is very bad then."

She nodded. "I will remember."

"Are you from Germany?"

"Oh, no. We are Swiss—like the chocolate!" she smiled. I laughed delighted. "Nice to meet you."

"The same." Still smiling, I left to find Jay.

He was at the microwave chatting to another tourist in what sounded like very fluent German to me. I gestured that I would stand in the checkout line. He joined me a couple of minutes later.

"Do you still have that list of numbers?" he murmured urgently.

I nodded.

"Give it to me."

I dug for it in my pocket. Jay waited with subdued excitement, grabbed it from my hand then hurried back to the tourist he'd been speaking to. I watched as he showed the numbers to the man, who studied them for a few seconds before shaking his head apologetically. Jay asked him another question. The man nodded, wrote down something and handed it to Jay with a smile. Jay thanked him warmly, shaking his hand. He was all but bouncing on his feet when he rejoined me. I looked at him askance.

"Tell you later." He winked, all mischievousness.

Jay seemed to enjoy keeping me in suspense, not saying much as we ate sausage rolls and drank coffee with enjoyment—the slightly greasy pastries and bitter coffee hitting just the right spot.

"So what is it? Is it a Swiss bank account number?" I finally asked; the suspense unbearable.

He shook his head grinning. "No. But it might be a Swiss Bank account password."

"You're kidding me!"

Jay's grin widened, "No wonder Henry's after it. Who knows how much money might be sitting in that account—and him with no password!"

"And Grierson," I reminded him. Grierson could be after it as well.

"Maybe," he shrugged. "Ready to go?"

* * *

We got to Winburg at dusk. Jay drove to a mall, pulling in near the movies. "Get your stuff—all your stuff. We're changing cars."

"Why?"

He paused, half-turning to me. "Grierson knows this one. Pointless going on with it."

"Yes, but..."

"Come on!" he urged, pulling at my bags.

Grumbling, I got out, reluctant to leave the safety the Pajero had come to represent. "What now? Take the bus?"

He just smiled. "Leave everything to me."

Leave everything to Jay. Five minutes later, a Landcruiser pulled up with a towering basketball player in the front and two noisy kids in the back. The driver jumped out, rushed up to Jay and gave him a big bear hug, saying, "Hey man! Long time *nosee!*"

"Took you long enough! Niko, this is Sammi. Sammi, Niko."

I remembered then that Jay's best school-friend had been Niko. He'd failed to tell me Niko lived in Winburg these days. I got a warm engulfing handshake.

"Come. Patty's waiting for you," invited Niko, opening the door to help throw our bags in.

The kids quietened down to stare at us. Jay waved. "Hello. You must be Kenny and Lisa."

"The very same," confirmed their father.

"They don't look like little devils."

"Wait till you get to know them!"

Jay helped me climb the high step. I smiled tentatively at Lisa. She looked about three. She stared, not smiling back. I tried the same smile with Kenny, who looked about six. He looked away immediately then looked back. I tried doing the same. He grinned. I grinned back.

Patty was pretty and easygoing, welcoming us like old friends. We immediately felt at home in their comfortable place. Dinner, a casserole, was served almost as soon as we arrived. It was a noisy, happy affair with the children getting used to us. They decided to entertain us with their stories and toys. Lisa took a shine to 'Uncle Jay', and kept trying to climb onto his lap to feed him.

"Leave Uncle Jay alone!" admonished her parents.

"S'okay," laughed Jay, handing her over to Patty.

The delicious meal was soon over, leaving a warm glow in my being. Patty began to clear the table. I got up too, offering to do the dishes.

"Oh no, the boys will do it. If they can't stack the dishwasher, we'll know they're next to useless!" declared Patty with a grin.

"Come with me. Let's see what's bugging you." I looked at her quizzically. "I was a nurse. I know when someone is trying to hide pain. Come." She led me to the bathroom. "Let's see."

I pulled my shirt up. The wound had stopped bleeding some time ago, but it still felt tender. Gently, Patty pulled away the untidy dressing to inspect the wound. Then she looked me in the eye.

"Who shot you?"

"An accountant."

She raised her eyebrows in surprise. "Do the police know?"

I nodded. Satisfied, she left it at that, tending the wound with cool, professional hands.

"You've got a lovely family," I told her.

"Yes. And you and Jay will have one, too." She smiled.

I laughed. "Oh no! We're just friends." She gave me a doubtful look. "Really," I added. "We've been friends forever. It's never been anything else."

She still maintained her doubtful look whilst sorting out my bandage. "Could have fooled me! He's running round the country protecting you now?"

I nodded, "But Jay's like that."

"And then there's the way he looks at you. I know these things. He's gonna marry you. And from what Niko tells me of him, you'll be a very lucky girl indeed. There!" She patted the dressing.

I was still stunned. "You've got it all wrong, Patty. It's not like that at all."

"We'll see," she said with a smile, leading the way back to the lounge for tea and coffees.

Niko and Jay were telling us how they'd almost blown up their school lab when I got a text from Mary. We'd agreed not to call unless absolutely necessary. 'Insp G says IntPol wants 2 spk with u. Call urgent!' went her text.

"Excuse me, I need to make a phone call," I explained, moving towards the hall.

"Hang on! Here are the keys." Niko threw them to Jay, who caught them easily and stood up.

"It's just a phone call." I looked at the men in confusion.

"We think it's better if you made it from a phone box," Jay said over his shoulder, on the way to the door.

"You're not serious!"

He shrugged. I exchanged a look with Patty. She shrugged too.

"Okay. Best not take any chances, I suppose."

***

We drove to a call-box by the mall. It was a card only.

"Dammit!" I exclaimed, wondering where on Earth to buy a card at that hour. Jay pulled out a card from his wallet. I stared at him in disbelief.

"Backup," he stated. "My phone's always running down."

Shaking my head, I dialled Mary's number. "Hi Mary, it's me. What's going on?"

"Hi sweetie, are you okay?"

"Yes. Jay's taking care of me. What's wrong?"

"Inspector Govender wants to talk to you. Says that Interpol has an interest in this case and has one of their men working on it—an Inspector Grierson."

I sighed, "Yes, I've met him."

"You have? His name is Terry Grierson."

"*Ja.* He's the spitting image of the guy from the labyrinth."

"Yes. They're brothers?"

"Identical."

"Twins!"

"He threatened Jay and me. I don't want to talk to him, but I'll call the Inspector."

"You do that, sweetie."

"Got to go. I'll keep you updated when I can."

"I'd like that."

We said goodbye.

"Need to talk to the inspector," I informed Jay as he lounged against the Landcruiser. He walked over to lean against the wall while I dialled.

"Hello, Inspector Govender?"

His guarded bass tones came down the line, "Yes?"

"It's Samantha Gonzales. Mary Stewart said I needed to call you."

"I'm glad you did. There's been a lot going on. It seems the man who died had contacted Interpol and was acting on their behalf. They want to talk to you."

"His brother?"

"Yes."

"What about Henry Wilkins?"

"He's disappeared. His office says he's away on business in America. Have you seen him or had any contact with him?"

"No. But he was at my sister's in Harties on Sunday afternoon."

That news was greeted with silence. Then, "You really should have told me earlier." The Inspector's displeasure could not have been more eloquent.

"Um...Sorry, but I wasn't thinking straight. There's.... something else." I glanced at Jay. He nodded encouragingly.

"Yes?"

"There was a slip of paper in the labyrinth. I think that's what Henry wants."

"What piece of paper?"

"It was in a little tube in the ground. I found it just before Grierson and Henry arrived; before the shooting."

"Why didn't you tell me about this?" demanded the inspector. "I could have you arrested for withholding evidence!"

Feeling horribly guilty, I did my best to explain. "I'd put it in my pocket when Grierson found me. And then I forgot about it. It's all printed. There's nothing to connect it to the shooting except my word, really."

"That's for me to decide. How do you know the decease's name?"

"His brother, the Interpol guy, has been threatening me and my friend."

The inspector's silence made it obvious I'd just ruined his night, if not his whole week.

"What friend?" he eventually asked.

I hesitated. Jay shrugged. He was thinking the same thing; Grierson of Interpol knew of him already. And Inspector Govender seemed to be more approachable and reasonable. "Jay Duart."

"Right." It sounded like he was writing it down. "Just keep out of Wilkins' way. And of Inspector Grierson's until I've spoken to him. You said he threatened you?"

"He threatened Jay and broke into Jay's house to question me...And he chased me."

"I see. His brother was killed. He shouldn't even be on this case. I'll talk to him. And you talk to me. Keep in touch, especially if Wilkins contacts you. Now, what does that piece of paper say?"

"It's just a list of numbers. My friend thinks it's a Swiss Bank account password."

The inspector muttered something about amateurs that sounded quite rude, but I couldn't quite catch it. "Okay. Give them to me."

I listed the numbers.

"Call me as soon as there are any developments," instructed the inspector.

I assured him I would before cutting the call.

Jay looked askance at me. "He'll talk to Grierson?"

I nodded.

"Then that's half the problem solved." He smiled.

I smiled back less cheerfully. I didn't think it was going to be that easy.

* * *

Patty sent us off the following morning with a huge hearty breakfast: eggs, toast, wors, hash-browns, pancakes, sausages, croissants —the whole works. It was better than Wimpy. Afterwards, Niko led us to the garage. He lifted the second wooden door reverently.

There stood an immaculate, shiny dark-blue metallic Mini Clubman with tinted windows.

Jay grinned broadly. "You've taken good care of her."

"Yep."

"You sure?" Jay watched Niko's face.

"It was a stupid bet, anyway." Niko sounded regretful, handing over the keys to Jay.

I looked at them both, mystified.

Niko explained. "I bet Jay he wouldn't be married by the age of 35. So, I've had the car for the past two years. Had always wanted a Mini."

"You mean it was Jay's?"

"Yep," answered Jay. "Bought it with some money from Mac4U."

He began packing the car with our stuff.

Mac4U had been the AppleMac technician service Jay had started after qualifying as a techie. He'd made obscene amounts of money setting up AppleMac networks and servicing them at a time when every little multimedia studio was switching to Mac. Jay had worked incredibly hard for just over four and a half years before suddenly selling the business and going off to study Microbiology. I vaguely wondered what his next career move would be.

We said goodbye to Niko then rolled down the drive, waving to Patty and the kids as they stood on the lawn shouting, "Come see us soon."

We mutely wound our way through the quiet holiday morning.

"They're such a lovely family," I finally broke the quiet, feeling all warm and fuzzy.

"Ja."

"Jay?"

"Hmm?"

"Thanks."

I wasn't quite sure what I was thanking him for, but he seemed to know anyway. He just smiled, and floored the accelerator sending us hurtling smoothly down the on-ramp to seamlessly join the highway.

~ 4 ~

CLARENS

We took the B-Road to join the Bethlehem one, the Mini making short work of the Free State hillsides and farmland with fields of tired sunflowers. Winter was approaching, parching the roadsides into dusty monotones while the strips of emerald irrigated fields stood lushly out. Jay and I fell into those silly nonsensical chats like the ones we'd often had at Tech. I'd forgotten how much I'd missed them, and how much we'd laughed until I'd gotten stitches. Mindful of my real stitches, I tried to subside into giggles.

"It's good to hear you laugh again," Jay remarked, sounding suddenly serious.

"We laugh on the phone—sometimes."

"*Ja.* But it's not the same."

He was right. It was far from being the same. "I expect it's because we're getting older."

"Mm. Then we should be laughing more."

I had to smile again.

We were about two hours from Clarens when I first noticed the black BMW just like Henry's. And it had Gauteng number-plates. Jay glanced at me, noticing immediately that I was tensing up.

"There's a black BMW X3 behind us," I replied tersely to his unspoken question.

He checked the rear-view mirror. "It's too far away to make out the driver." Jay glanced at me again. "Don't freak out, okay."

"What...?"

He was already slowing down and indicating, pulling us over onto the gravel shoulder.

"Jay!" I couldn't help *but* freak out, hyperventilating. Didn't he have any idea how dangerous this was?

He brought us to a halt, turned off the engine and switched on the hazards saying, "It'll be alright. Trust me." Then he was opening his door and stepping out.

"Jay!"

The BMW was almost on us now, with no other traffic in sight. Jay popped the bonnet. I ducked as the BMW swished by. A few seconds passed. Jay fidgeted under the hood before shutting it. The BMW was disappearing around a curve.

He slid back in and started the engine. "Did you see the driver?"

"No. I ducked down."

"It was a man. Wore sunglasses. Couldn't see much. What does Henry look like?"

I tried to picture Henry. "He's a little taller than you. Dark hair, brown eyes. Wears metal-frame glasses. He's very thin with a long face...and very pale, like he doesn't get much sun. A straight nose and neat eyebrows, but thick. Very nerdish looking."

"Right," was all he said putting on his own sunglasses. And we were off again, no sign of the BMW—like it had never been.

* * *

Clarens greeted us in the late afternoon with its peacefulness and beauty almost; foreign in its nature, like visiting another little country. After popping into the Spar, we found a little cottage for the night, sitting just under a mountain at the end of a dirt road. Just up the track, we were told by Magda the owner, was an excellent good bookstore. I shivered and nodded politely. It was freezing!

"Let it snow, let it snow...," sang Jay. I couldn't help but join in as we walked with Magda to the cottage.

"Oh, you never know," said Magda with a smile, opening the door and showing us in, then gave us the standard holiday cottage spiel. She ended with, "If there's anything you need, just let me know. I can see you two are going to just love it here. Not many couples that don't!" She left with another naughty smile.

Jay and I exchanged an awkward look.

"Flip you for the bed," I eventually suggested. He nodded. "Heads or tails?"

"Neither," he replied.

"No, seriously."

"Seriously."

"Jay!"

He sighed. "If it's neither, I'll take the sofa."

I stared at him. He stared back.

"Okay," I shrugged.

The coin bounced onto its edge, rolled drunkenly towards the door and onto the doorstop. There it appeared to be magnetised, standing upright. I stood gaping. What were the odds! Jay knelt down to give the coin an experimental wiggle with the tip of his finger.

"Well, I'll be!" he finally remarked sardonically.

"I'll—,"

But he'd already gotten up and was heading for the bedroom. "I'll get the bedding. You get supper."

There wasn't much to do. Just shove the stuff we'd bought into the microwave, and lay out plates and cutlery.

He was back in two minutes with an armful of bedding. Throwing it onto the only armchair, he went over to the fireplace and started building a fire. The temperature was dropping steadily.

"Do you want the TV on?" He sounded distracted.

"No, it's fine. Don't feel like watching anything." I still felt a bit awkward, not quite able to figure why.

Jay soon got the fire going. It was burning pleasantly, making the room feel nice and cosy, when I brought over the plates and mugs to the coffee table.

"Thanks." Jay didn't look at me as he took his plate of ribs, spinach and feta, and butternut. Another plate held the Portuguese rolls. Feeling unusually self-conscious, I told myself not to be so silly as I took my place next to him on the two-seater sofa. I picked up a rib and gnawed on it.

"Hmm. These are good!" I remarked, enjoying the sweet, tangy sauce.

"Hmm hmm. So's the spinach."

I relaxed. It was peaceful in the room with the cheerful, patient crackle of the fire and Jay's reassuring presence. The silence was companionable. But Jay had something to say.

"Sammi?" he eventually began, halfway through his plate.

"Hmm? Do you want it heated up?" I held out a hand for his plate.

"Er...no. I was just wondering...,"

I looked at him expectantly.

"How come you haven't found a guy yet—you know, to settle down with?

I put the rib down on my plate, buying some time to frame my thoughts and for an answer that would make sense. I sighed, then said, "I don't know...I just haven't found the right guy yet. One I'd be happy to spend the rest of my life with...And I've been busy, too —with my career. Or rather, trying to keep my head above water, you know. There just always seemed like there was loads of time to meet the right guy. I didn't expect it to fly by so fast; for it to take so long to get my career on-track."

"*Ja*, I know," he began. "But time's ticking fast now. If you really want to settle down, you should be doing so soon."

I stared at him, hurt and a little angry, horribly aware he was only voicing my own fears. "Are you trying to say that I'm too old; that I'm going to be an old maid!"

"Well, technically, you are an old maid." he smiled.

I glared at him.

"Sammi, I just mean that...Maybe you should stop waiting. Maybe you should marry someone who doesn't match up absolutely with that list in your head."

"What list in my head?"

"The one every girl has of the guy she wants to marry. Because soon all you'll have is a career, which doesn't pay the best and won't comfort you in your old age. You'll always be replaceable to an employer, and a lot of guys may not...pay you as much attention," he finished gently.

I stared at him appalled, feeling more hurt than if all this had come from my mum or one of my aunts. "Are you saying that no-one will want to marry me 'cos I'm too old?" My voice sounded harsh even to me.

"No, no!" he turned to face me, having to save his fork as it tried to fall off. "I'm just...Look, you're still gorgeous and any guy would be lucky to marry you, but maybe you should settle for *any* guy and not *the* guy, okay?"

"So, I should marry the first guy who asks me?" I felt hot with betrayal.

"No, no, that's not..."

"That's rich coming from you, Mr I-never-commit-to-anything-except-my-Pajero!"

He gave me a level look. "Okay. You know what? Let's forget this, okay?"

"Okay."

"Good."

"Good."

"You gonna eat that?"

"No, you can have it. There."

"Thanks."

We settled back to munching again, nothing else left to say to each other.

* * *

An hour later, with the dishes done, I said goodnight to Jay and went to bed, still hurt by his statement that I was an old maid. And sure more than ever that Patty was wrong. I wasn't even Jay's type.

I tossed and turned for a while.

Unbidden, I remembered our one and only class trip to Johannesburg. We'd ended the night at a karaoke club. I didn't sing. Jay did—a Letters To Cleo song. He'd sung with that raw, tongue-in-cheek neediness, putting on a superb performance, mugging to the microphone like Damon Albarn mugging Liam Gallagher. I'd thought it as hysterical as everyone else, at first. Then came the bit towards the end where he seemed to be singing it especially for me. He caught my gaze, holding it intently, not bopping around at all, whether as part of his act or not, I couldn't quite figure out. I'd been left standing rather bemused as he ended his act by moshing into the small crowd that had gotten up to cheer in front of him. I'd tried to convince myself it was just my imagination. He hadn't been trying to tell me anything special. He must have just gotten fully into the whole act.

Then he was back, moving towards me, laughing excitedly, on a high from all the compliments and exertion. He started to say something to me, but was mobbed by a party of girls before he could get out more than, "Sammi..!" He seemed to be enjoying the attention, so I let myself be dragged to the Ladies by Liesl, convinced by then it had all just been some weird effect that had made me read so much into the song. Scolding myself for being so silly, I was also laughing at myself. He was just being Jay, right?

~ 5 ~

INTRUSION

I woke up early the next morning, reluctant to jump out of bed in the pre-dawn chill. Soon after, I heard shuffling in the other room before Jay knocked on the door softly.

"You up?"

"Hmm."

"Just going for a run."

"Hmm." I felt too drowsily warm and snug to bother replying further or to move from the comfortable bed.

There was the soft click of the door closing, then the dark shape of Jay through the curtain as he walked across the lawn. I drowsed for a while oblivious of time. The snick of the door opening came sooner than expected. Wondering if Jay would mind putting off our departure by an hour or two, I half-turned in anticipation of his knock on the bedroom door again. It didn't come.

I raised myself on my elbow almost certain I'd heard the door open and close. Had I dreamt it? Puzzled, I listened intently. There it was—the barely perceptible sound of soft soles on the tiles. A stealthy sound. What was Jay up to? The bathroom door creaked open. I lay back again. Jay was just going to take a shower. He would get me up when he was done. I settled down to drowse some more. Something was wrong...I couldn't hear any water running.

With the beginnings of alarm, I pulled on my sweater and boots. *There was no way Henry or Grierson could have found me, right?* There was no way they could have traced the Mini so quickly. Besides, Henry was in America. So, that just left a thief. I looked around for a weapon and my cellphone. Slipping the phone into my pocket, I contemplated the heavy art deco lamp for a moment before I went to unplug it. *But what if they had guns or knives?* My eye was caught by the pot-pourri balls. They looked like marbles. Carrying the bowl carefully to the door, I inched it open to peep through.

Henry stood gazing back at me, his gun unwavering. I froze, petrified. The seconds ticked by as we stared at each other. He moved forward with determination. Taking a step back with a gasp, not even thinking, I flung the bowl at him and slammed the door shut, locking it. Henry swore, then swore again, crashing about the hall. I was already through the French windows, running out.

It was shockingly cold outside. I ran frantically towards Magda's home, my steps scrunching on the frosty grass. I almost made it, too. Just at Magda's doorstep, I was grabbed around the waist and lifted off the ground. A hand clamped over my mouth, blocking my scream. He dragged me back towards the cottage. I struggled, but his grip just tightened till I almost couldn't breathe.

Grierson threw me onto the sofa then shut the door. "Where is he?"

I was still gasping for breath.

"Is he here?" he demanded again, pulling out a gun.

I nodded. "He's...here. Henry's outside." I finally got out.

"What?"

"Henry's here. With a gun. I think he's still outside."

Grierson stood, unseeing, thinking. I realised then the 'he' Grierson had meant was Jay. He hadn't expected Henry to be here any more than I had.

"Stay there!"

He moved rapidly, going through the cottage. His quick steps told me he was checking the bathroom and then the bedroom. I'd just started to move when he got back.

He looked at me, a warning in his eye. "Where's you friend?"

"I don't know." His eyes narrowed. "He went for a run." I almost tripped over my words. His eyes were still distrustful, maybe even vengeful.

"At this time of the morning?"

What could I say, except, "Well, he's obviously not here!" I didn't think he'd appreciate the sarcasm. I was right.

He gave me an annoyed look which quickly turned into one of assessment. "You're clearly not stupid, so let's not beat around the bush. What's Henry up to?"

"How should I know? I'm the one he's trying to kill!"

"Don't give me that! I know you're helping him!"

His angry eyes bore into me. I cowered, trying to make some space between me and that tower of rage, bewildered that he thought I had anything to do with Henry. "Look," I tried, willing my voice to stop shaking. "I'm so sorry about your brother..." I didn't know what else to say to placate him. Maybe that wasn't the wisest thing...

"He wouldn't have died if it weren't for you two." he growled.

I stared at him, dumbfounded.

"You're Henry's accomplice, aren't you? You double-crossed him. Now, he's after you. And I'm not letting you out of my sight until I make him pay!"

I opened my mouth trying to think of something that would make him realise how wrong he'd gotten it. His glare was unwavering. Whatever I said would be a waste of breath. He had the look of a man who, once he'd decided something was true, would never be swayed. But I had to try. "I'm not Henry's accomplice. I hadn't even met him until Thursday evening!"

"Then what were you doing at the labyrinth?"

"I was...meditating."

"You must meditate a lot. On Thursday night after you were apparently too tired to socialise. And again on Friday morning. He'd raised his eyebrows sarcastically.

"Your brother attacked me on Thursday night." I burst out, instantly regretting it.

"He attacked you? Lionel attacked *you*?"

I nodded dispiritedly.

"Lionel would never hurt a lady...Why? Did you attack him?" His eyes were dangerous little slits.

My heartbeat raced, knowing I was getting out of the pot and into the fire. I took a deep breath and shook my head well aware he was standing there like a ticking bomb; one I couldn't help but detonate. "I went down to the labyrinth that night expecting to have a peaceful meditation. He was by the centre stone. I didn't see him at first. He was in the shadows. It was only when I got closer that I realised something was wrong, and I got scared. I started to run away, but slipped and fell. He caught me, demanding to know what I was doing there...He was hurting me. I tried to fight him off, managed to get free and...ran away..."

He hadn't taken those eyes off me, still tense, ready to explode. "And on Friday?" His voice was soft, almost a whisper.

I took another deep breath, dropping my eyes, not wanting to look at those eyes. "When he found me at the labyrinth. He was...angry at me."

"Did you hurt him on Thursday?"

I glanced up to meet his eyes. I had to look away almost immediately. "I think I might have kicked him."

"I bet you did."

"He asked me who Henry was. Henry started to run down to the labyrinth."

"You were meeting Henry there?"

"No! I told you, I went to meditate.

"Oh right. You went there to meditate."

"Yes." My chin was sticking out with defiance, my anger returning.

"Go on."

"When I got to the centre stone, I could see a little tube sticking out, and I started to dig it out. Henry came along and I told him I wanted to be alone. He went away. He came back when he saw me talking to your brother. I thought he was going to save me..."

"He arrived just after Lionel. How convenient."

"He was probably watching the labyrinth from the trees." It was obvious Grierson didn't believe a word. He still looked ready to explode.

In the tense silence, the sound of running steps on gravel could be heard. I stared at the door, afraid it might be Henry. It was Jay. He flung open the door, stopped for an instant, covered in sweat, chest heaving. Grierson had half turned to watch the door. Jay launched himself, striking out at Grierson's face. But Grierson had dropped to the floor, dodging Jay's knee, to punch him hard in the stomach. Rising up swiftly, Grierson struck Jay twice with his elbows. Jay hit the floor unconscious.

"Jay!" I was half-way to Jay's side when I was jerked back by my collar and hurled back onto the sofa.

"Don't move!"

Tears blurred my sight and I blinked them away rapidly. Jay looked all crumpled and vulnerable, unmoving. A few seconds ticked by. "Is he dead?" I whispered.

"Not yet!" growled Grierson. He made to move to Jay when the window shattered with a shock. Grierson dived down again. Belatedly, I spread myself flat on the sofa, covering my head as if it would help. More shots were fired. I screamed as Grierson grabbed me, pulling me off the sofa. He hauled me by my arm painfully, forcing me to crawl along with him out the door.

"Jay!" I cried.

But Jay was still unconscious.

~ 6 ~

GOLDEN GATE

Once again I found myself being manhandled by a Grierson into a confrontation with Henry, dragged along stumbling and sailing at the end of his hand like a gybing boom on a yacht.

Around the cottage we went, and almost into Henry. For a second it was *deja vu* with a Grierson squaring off to Henry, warily looking down the barrel of the accountant's gun. Henry obviously thought so too. His eyes widened as he took an involuntary step back in shock. It lasted all of a couple of seconds. His gun steadied. It was happening again!

I tensed in anticipation of Grierson's heavy body falling onto mine. But this Grierson wasn't about to underestimate Henry. This Grierson had a gun. And stood much closer. He deflected Henry's gun, bringing up his knee. But Henry, showing amazing anticipation, leapt back, turned tail and ran off. Grierson, never letting go of me, started after him.

A few metres on, Henry half-swung back to fire blindly.

We dived to the ground, the grass, dry and painfully poky, breaking under our weight. Grierson fired a couple of deliberate shots at Henry who was already disappearing into the trees. Then, we were up and running towards Grierson's Audi. There was a slam of a car door followed by the almost instant sound of the engine roaring into life. The black BMW erupted from the trees spewing gravel our way and at the Audi we had just reached. I was forced, almost exhausted, into the passenger seat. Grierson hopped across the bonnet and into the car. We were off before I'd even got my breath back.

Engine gunned, we raced up to the town square, turning left then left again to head off down the hill to the main road. The BMW was in sight now, at the T-junction turning right. It almost hit a *bakkie* heading towards Harrismith. The *bakkie* braked heavily. Heedlessly, Henry sped off towards the Golden Gate National Park.

Grierson barely stopped at the T-junction. A minute later we'd overtaken the same *bakkie* and were gaining on the BMW. What did Grierson plan to do once he caught up with Henry? Was I going to witness another murder? I glanced at Grierson. His expression was inscrutable. "What will you do once you catch him?" I spoke more to distract myself from the fantastically dangerous speeds at which we were travelling than from any burning desire to know.

"That depends on him," was the terse reply.

We were almost on the BMW when we flew past Kiara Lodge, rounded the bend and raced straight for the checkpoint, clear of any other traffic. Henry gave no sign of slowing down or stopping. Grierson changed shifted down a gear then floored the accelerator. The Audi gained on the BMW, but not enough. A hapless guard waved his clipboard at us before having to jump out of the way. We were almost level with Henry; and the gatehouse. I opened my mouth to scream, certain I was going to be crushed into that stone-work. Grierson swerved around onto the lane for oncoming traffic. We shot passed the gatehouses, Henry barely a nose in front of us.

Then we were speeding alongside him, beginning to pull ahead of the BMW. He swerved, attempting to ram us into the rocky hillside. Grierson, forced to avoid him, tried to stay off the rocky shoulder. We rounded a bend with us on the inside, on the on-coming lane. A Baz Bus was rushing cheerfully towards us. Grierson braked hard, nipping in inches behind the BMW. The Baz Bus driver hooted angrily but we were already rounding the next sixty degree bend, sitting on Henry's tail. Petrified, I didn't dare steal a look at the speedometer or at Grierson. The Audi hugged the bends like some expensive car ad. I didn't want to be in any ad. I wanted to be safe in the Mini with Jay.

The BMW suddenly swerved into a lay-by at a viewpoint, braking hard. We overshot him.

Grierson slammed on the brakes, taking the next curve badly, half trying to see what Henry was up to. The BMW had raced up to our tail. He rammed us, shoving us into the next curve—a hairpin. Above the sound of our screeching tyres, I heard someone shrieking from what seemed like far away. It was me.

The Audi, all traction lost, slid to the side, almost onto the BMW. A whirl of green, brown, and grey earth streamed in front of us. Grierson stopped fighting the wheel, turning into the slide and accelerating. We did a one-eighty degree spin, rocking to a halt seconds later, inches from a huge boulder.

I remembered to take a breath.

"You alright?" Grierson was breathing heavily, too.

I nodded, unable to speak even if I wanted to. Henry had disappeared.

"Dammit!" Terry Grierson exploded, thumping the wheel. He took a deep breath before dialling his cellphone. There was no reception.

A three-point turn later, we were headed for Qwa-Qwa and Harrismith.

* * *

"What do you know about the road?"

I took a minute to remember the map. "Not much. There's Qwa-Qwa, then Harrismith."

"Any turnings off the major road?" Typically, Grierson seemed to have no map with him.

"I think there's the alternative route to Durban. The Oliviershoek Pass and Sterkfontein Dam road."

"What's it like, do you know?"

"Jay said it was like the Golden Gate with more massive potholes than tar. He wasn't going to take it."

"Ah. Jay."

I didn't like his tone.

"You do keep some interesting company, don't you Samantha Gonzales?"

"What's that suppose to mean?"

He smiled grimly. "Just that two of the men in your recent company have been known to commit serious international crimes."

My face flushed hotly. "I didn't choose to be in Henry's or your company."

He looked at me in slight surprise. "You think I'm a criminal?"

"You act like one!"

He smiled crookedly, a bit of meanness creeping in. "I didn't mean myself. I meant your 'friend' Jay."

I glared at him. "Jay's no criminal!"

"Oh, really? That's not what the files at Interpol say."

"I don't believe you!"

"What do you know about Jay's life between 2000 and 2003?"

"He was travelling and working abroad."

"That's right. A drifter with some very interesting friends. Like Thomas MacKenzie, also known as Ha Sibh Ken."

"Am I supposed to know that name?" I feared he going to tell me the guy was some sort of terrorist.

"He was the most successful hacker back then. Hacked into numerous governments and UN servers."

"Doesn't that happen all the time," I tried to sound bored.

"No." He changed down, overtaking a Mazda. We slid back into the lane effortlessly. "MacKenzie left little notes of what he thought of the government scrawled across confidential files. Then he transferred funds, reallocating them to projects he deemed more worthy."

"Like what?"

"He took two billion from a defence budget and reallocated it to health, education and the environment."

"Can I vote for him?" I liked the sound of this guy, MacKenzie. But Grierson didn't share my views.

"It's a serious crime. It took months to sort out and a lot of manpower. They are still sorting out some aspects of it."

"What 's Jay got to do with it?"

"Rumour is MacKenzie didn't do it all himself. Jay is believed to have helped him plan and execute the whole thing. He may have stolen passwords and set up diversions."

"May have?" I jumped on it, not believing my ears. Although reallocating funds to needy programs sounded just like Jay...We'd even joked about doing something similar once, back when we were students. A what-if that would never happen.

"He was never fully implicated. MacKenzie didn't sell out his friends."

"Jay is probably totally innocent."

"That he most certainly is not!" Grierson's voice had gotten grim again. "During that period, he was also arrested for breaking a man's back in a bar in Germany. Pleaded not guilty. Got clean away. Has the luck of the devil, wouldn't you say?"

"I don't believe you! Jay would never do such a thing. He doesn't even like bars!"

"I could show you the file."

I gave him a suspicious look. *What was he up to?* "You've got it all wrong. Your judgement is way off. For heaven's sake, you think I'm in league with Henry! As far as I can see, you're full of BS!"

"My, aren't we the loyal one. You must truly love him."

I stared out the window, unseeing. "He's my best friend."

* * *

Grierson said nothing as I sat there in a whirl of emotions. Something about Grierson's revelations was bothering me. Why was he blackening Jay? Did he think Jay had something to do with this whole affair? Absolutely absurd! It was me who'd gotten Jay involved in this whole mess. And Jay was one of the mellowest persons I knew. He wasn't known for resorting to violence. Humour and absurdly strange behaviour—yes; violence—no. He almost never lost his temper. Unbidden, a half remembered scene from Tech played back in my mind; the first and only time I'd seen Jay lose his temper.

I hadn't caught how it had all started or why. All I saw was Mike flying through the air in the lecture room, seemingly linked to Jay's fingers. Mike hit the first tier of seats hard. Then Jay was stepping forward, still holding onto Mike's hand, twisting it down and against the seats, a focused look on his face. A short sharp kick, the snap of bone, and Mike's scream. A stunned silence as everyone stared speechless, myself included. Jay had been breathing hard, still furious. He turned on his heel and brushed past me. I tried to follow him, still shaky, but he'd moved too fast down the hall and disappeared around the corner. I didn't think he wanted to be around people just then. He'd never said why he'd broken Mike's arm. Only that he hadn't really meant too—that he'd lost his temper. All Mike had said was that he'd rather be in a car crash than in a fight with Jay; and had given him a wide berth from then on.

Grierson was saying something. "Hmm...what?" My mind was still back at Tech.

"For what it's worth, Samantha, I don't think you're a criminal."

"Oh, well. Thank you!" I tried to keep the stiffness out of my voice. "What changed your mind?"

"You've had any number of opportunities to help Henry over the past hour. And you haven't. So either you are seriously double-crossing him, or you're not involved with him at all."

"What makes you think I'm not double-crossing him?" *Why did I always have to play devil's advocate?*

His reply was simple. "You don't seem the type."

"Took you long enough to see!"

He smiled at me, a brilliant sincere smile. I couldn't help but smile back despite my misgivings.

"So what can you tell me about Jay?" he asked casually, confirming my misgivings.

I didn't quite know how to handle it, so I stalled. "You seem to know more about him than I do, or so you claim. What else could you possibly want to know?"

"Everything." He was looking straight ahead again, that intent look returning. "Convince me he's not a criminal."

I gave him a wary look. He smiled again, that incredibly attractive smile. The kind that made hearts do flip-flops...I looked away quickly, telling myself it was just stress and worry that was making my heart beat so fast. Eventually, I said, "He's the kindest, mellowest person I know. A bit strange at times but in a nice way, not a psycho way."

"Any girlfriends?"

I had to think a bit. "One or two. None serious, especially since he started studying again. Had his heart broken a few years ago. Still getting over it."

"Who was she?"

I tried not to show my surprise and renewed unease. I didn't want to give Grierson anything he could use against Jay, seeing how the man seemed to have it in for him.

"Trish." I wasn't going to give him any more.

"And what about you?" went on Grierson, suddenly changing tack. "Any significant others. Or exes?"

I shot him another suspicious look. "None of your business!" It really was none of his business. *Impertinent, Arrogant...*

He was laughing. "I suppose it isn't. I'm just trying to get to know you better. You've piqued my interest."

Gone was the menacing man who'd put me in danger and accused me of felonies. Instead, I saw a charming, attractive man who, it seemed, was attempting to flirt with me!

"Go on. Tell me who the real Samantha Gonzales is," cajoled Grierson.

"I will if you tell me who you really are, Inspector Grierson."

He was quiet for a minute or two. "Fine. It's a deal. I'm Terence Grierson, thirty-nine. My friends and family call me Terry. You can, too. I've worked for Interpol for the last five years, mostly in organised crime. Never been married. No family, now that Lionel's gone. Our parents died in a car crash in '79, and grandpa and ma have both passed away."

"I'm sorry."

He didn't seem to hear. Most of his attention appeared to be on the road. Talking in a soft, reflective voice, he continued, "Hobbies: books, collecting modern art, travelling. Sports: Judo, Hapkido and swimming. Likes: Good food and wine. Dislikes: bad drivers and criminals. Right! Your turn!" And he shot me a challenging smile.

"Okay. I'm Samantha Gonzales. Middle child with an older brother and younger sister—both married. But not me. You'll know I'm thirty-three already. I work as a DTP Designer for a medium-sized ad agency..."

"Do you like it?"

"*Ja*, most of the time. But I actually want to be a healer and therapist. I study that when I can."

"Ah. Mary Stewart," came the cynical remark.

I half turned toward him. "So, I take it you don't believe in energy healing?"

"Or psychics. Don't change the subject. Go on about yourself."

We were speeding past Qwa-Qwa now, the veld turning brown in-between row upon row of blocks of cement houses. Terry swerved nonchalantly around a bull standing in the middle of the road, giving me a few moments to consider how much of myself I should reveal to this man.

"Hobbies: reading, movies, energy healing. Likes: children, winter and ice-cream. Dislikes: arrogant bastards who try to bully everyone."

"Ouch! I take it you mean me."

I didn't bother to reply, keeping my eyes on a pair of hawks circling a field.

He tried again, "So tell me..." His phone rang. Decelerating to pull over onto the shoulder of the road, he answered the call, "Grierson." The phone squawked at him along with bursts of static, signalling a storm somewhere not too far away. He spoke in his terse way, "I found Wilkins in Clarens."

Hardly, more like he happened by...

"He's in a black BMW X3, registration GP123456. I lost him in Golden Gate. He tried to kill me."

He hadn't mentioned he had me with him. I was just about to say something, thinking it prudent to let at least one other person know I was with Grierson, but I was too late.

He was already saying, "Call me when you locate him." He cut the call and we were off again.

~ 7 ~

LADYSMITH

"Tell me about energy healing. You seem intelligent. How could you possibly believe in it?"

Grierson grinned as I gawked at him and his double-edged compliment.

"You can read about it yourself!"

"Come on! We've got some time. Convince me."

"I don't think that's possible."

"Try me."

I sighed, wondering where to begin. "Okay. You know all living things have an electrical field or magnetic field—an energy field. It's a proven scientific fact."

He nodded, "I know."

"Well, energy healing influences this field. It balances the field out and helps strengthen it so that the being is in a perfect state: mentally, physically and spiritually."

"Hmm..."

To my utter lack of surprise, he still wasn't convinced. "When you're sick, depressed, or stressed, your energy field is weakened. Sometimes it even has holes where your energy leaks out. So you feel drained; no energy to do anything, right?"

He nodded again. "Right."

"So the energy healer tries to seal these holes as well as clear out any negative energy. Then, they try to increase and encourage the flow and circulation of positive energy thereby healing the sickness and other complaints."

"Sounds great. What do you do? A spell?"

"No. You sweep the energy field, or aura, with your hands. You channel energy or help the person channel their own energy. There's no magic or spells involved."

"Sounds simple. Almost too simple."

"It *is* simple but it takes practice and dedication to do it effectively."

He still didn't look convinced. "Tell me about psychics."

I suddenly felt overwhelmingly exhausted. "No, I'm going to get some sleep now." I shut my eyes and tried a few energy visualisations. I was asleep within a minute or two.

I awoke, disturbed by a flash of light, after what seemed like five minutes. Thunder followed almost immediately, loud enough to shake the car. We were just entering Van Reenen's Pass. 'Welcome to KwaZulu-Natal' read the sign.

Terry kept to the outside lane, driving sedately at the 80km per hour speed limit as we began winding our way down. Visibility was bad—typical. Van Reenen's either had very good visibility or very bad; there wasn't any in-between.

"Feeling better?" asked Terry, his voice half-drowned by another ominous roll of thunder.

I shook my head. "No." I felt thirsty with that cotton-wool like feel in my head.

He shot me a quick glance. "We'll stop once we get down this pass. Get something to drink."

"That would be nice."

In seconds, we were driving through the brunt of the storm. It had turned into one of those amazingly violent and loud storms. Rain fell like a waterfall, accompanied by forked blue lightning with the occasional drum of hail. Fortunately, the wind wasn't too strong.

Trucks, and most cars, were pulling over to the shoulder, hazards blinking. Terry wasn't one of them, slowing us to a crawl instead, depending on the hazards, tyres and brakes of the car. Admittedly, they all seemed very good, but I wished he'd pulled over.

A torturous forty minutes later saw us leaving the pass. The worst of the storm was behind us, but the rain, much diminished, followed still. Terry started to accelerate, then remembered his promise and took us into the Engen 1-Stop.

"Five minutes," he said, hopping out of the car.

"Great." I found the energy to drag myself off to the Ladies.

* * *

Feeling slightly more human whilst washing my hands, I glanced up into the mirror. I wouldn't have recognised myself. My hair, usually trendily untidy, was plastered to my forehead except for some tufts sticking up. My eyes were sunken, dark-ringed and very cloudy. My lips looked dry and cracked, drawn into a tight line. The points of my jaw stood out prominently. I hadn't realised I'd been clenching it. Self-consciously, I tried to make myself relax. I started pulling funny-faces at the mirror.

"Samantha," called Terry, indicating my five minutes were up.

A spark of rebellion flared in my eyes, putting back a little light. Quickly, I splashed some cold water onto my face, hoping it would brighten up my pale, waxen skin.

"Samantha!" There was no doubt it was a command this time.

I stuck my head under the drier, drowning him out for half a minute, the hot air, blissfully soothing on my tense muscles. Then, and only then, did I leave the Ladies.

Terry was waiting outside in the drizzle, the familiar glower on his face. "Five minutes, I said."

"Surely you know that's impossible for us women," I replied sweetly.

Growling something under his breath, Terry opened the Audi door for me, more to make certain I got in than from any form of courtesy. The car felt nice and warm with the divine smell of coffee coming from the two steaming take-away cups. Two bottles of water, sat in my foot-well. Terry Grierson, it appeared, was very organised. He'd even thought of chips—just out of the oven—adding a salty tang to the aroma in the car. My tummy growled, reminding me I hadn't had any breakfast. Very, very organised was Terry Grierson. I neglected to tell him how impressed I was.

Terry put the Audi into gear and off we went again, accelerating towards Ladysmith. I wolfed down my share of the heavenly chips, starting to feel more like myself, then savoured the coffee.

* * *

"I've been thinking," began Terry, holding out the crumpled serviette he'd wiped his hands on.

I let him drop it into the carrier bag with the other remnants of the meal, hoping he wasn't going to bring up Jay again.

He didn't. "How did Henry find you?"

"I don't know. How did *you* find me?"

"Cellphone trace."

"But I didn't even make a call!"

"We have ways of tracking cellphones."

I was horrified. "Is it legal? Isn't it an invasion of my privacy?"

"It's part of an investigation that's bigger than you can imagine." His voice was flat.

I took that obtuse reply as a: 'It's not legal, but...'. My anger was rising again. "Maybe he also traced me by my cellphone...Or maybe he's psychic."

He was thoughtful for a few moments. "If Wilkins is tracking your phone then he knows where you are right now, but there's no sign of him."

"Maybe he's ahead. Or avoiding you."

"Hmm...Do you have your cellphone on you now?"

"*Ja*," I looked at him warily.

"Just wondering."

I didn't like his tone at all. It reminded me of fishermen and worms. I didn't want to be the bait.

"If you're even thinking of—" I never got a chance to complete that sentence. The driver's-side front tyre blew.

We slewed onto the oncoming lane, a big Toyota *bakkie* heading right for us. The man in the load-box raised his gun again. Terry fought the wheel, doing his best to keep us clear and slow us down. The second right-side tyre exploded as the *bakkie* was about to pass us.

"Get down!"

I ducked as a hail of bullets starred the windows, that now familiar feeling of imminent death taking over me; if not from the car crash then definitely from those men shooting at us. The Audi was now spinning to a halt as Terry spun the wheel instead of fighting it. I felt us hit the shoulder and skid onto gravel.

"Get out!" commanded Terry, leaning over my hunched shoulders to throw my door open.

Before I could move, he hit my seatbelt release and shoved me out. I fell out on all fours, the gravel cutting into my palms and knees.

Terry was scrambling out after me. "Come on!"

I was aware the *bakkie* was reversing. They were going to kill us. I felt numb.

"Move!" barked Terry.

Having leapt over me, he grabbed my arm and hauled me into the bushes, the thorn trees fighting to hold us painfully back.

We ran for a minute or two then abruptly stopped behind an anthill almost as tall as my shoulder. We listened, Terry's face once more intent, inscrutable. I leaned against his hard shoulder feeling more worn and exhausted than scared.

There were two of them from the *bakkie*, both with guns, travelling in a parallel line. One of the them was heading right for our little anthill. Terry shifted almost imperceptibly on his feet. I tried to move out of his way in anticipation of his moving, thinking he was probably going to shoot the guy. He waited until the man was almost to us before he kicked up and away through the top of the anthill into the man's face. The man screamed as the ants and sand hit him, dropping his gun to claw frantically at his face. Terry, clutching my arm again, pulled me away from the seething ants and back towards the road, picking up the gun on the way. We ran, keeping low. At the edge of the bushes before the shoulder, we stopped.

"Stay here." Terry was already slipping away, gun held like a baton.

'Here' was behind a twisted acacia bent over so the thorned branches almost formed a curtain to the road. I hunkered down, listening for the *bakkie* or, more hopefully, another car I could flag down. Nothing happened for a long agonising few minutes.

Terry's yelled order cut shockingly through the relative quiet. A surprised answering shout was followed by a single shot. The scream of the hurt man cut off sharply.

My heart stilled, afraid it was Terry who'd been shot, leaving me alone with those two men from the *bakkie*. I remained by the acacia, petrified, straining with my whole being to hear. A car was approaching. I couldn't decide whether to try to flag it down or not. I didn't know if I could. My limbs felt like stone—heavy, cold stone—immovable. The car sped by with a whoosh. Before I could berate myself, I heard the *bakkie* approaching.

Despite my apparent immobility, I managed to hunker down even more. A large man got out. He looked like a farmer with a *beer-boep* and a *bokkie-baard*. The man looked carefully around. Reaching into the *bakkie*, he took out a pistol and a bush-knife. Holding the weapons, one in each hand, he moved with cautious towards the bushes. He almost reached them, too.

Terry erupted from some bushes, slamming the rifle into Bakkie-man's midriff. In the same movement, he crouched down and swung at the back of the man's knees. Bakkieman hit the gravel with a thump, loosening his grip on his weapons. Terry was already lifting the rifle butt high to bring it down onto the man's upper chest. He kicked away the weapons from the man, then slammed him with the gun again as the man started to move.

"Samantha!" he called urgently. He didn't even sound winded.

I stood up shaking, shocked at such violence, but curiously elated that Terry was fine. I walked stiffly over, trembling almost uncontrollably, as Terry bent to confiscate the gun and the knife.

Next he took out his phone. "This is Inspector Grierson of Interpol. Police, ambulance and tow-truck to N3 Southbound, about 25ks out of Tugela Engen One-Stop..."

I stared, strangely detached, at Bakkieman. He was breathing with difficulty and quite unconscious. I wondered how the other two had fared.

Terry ended his call. "They'll be here in five minutes. Tracking helicopters are already on their way." Then he was gently hugging me, soothing my hair. "It's going to be okay," he murmured reassurance.

I didn't believe him. I didn't want this man touching me. I just wanted to be as far away from it all as possible.

* * *

The police, ambulance and tow-trucks arrived soon after. The man whom Terry had shot was loaded into an ambulance, bleeding profusely, along with his friend from the anthill who had blood all over his face. Bakkieman was loaded into another ambulance. I heard the paramedics diagnose him as having a few broken ribs, as I sat in the police car, covered in a blanket, drinking extremely sweet tea. The curiously detached feeling was still with me. I watched everything as if it was a movie on late night TV-- one you felt too tired to switch off even though you'd rather head off to bed.

Terry approached.

Crouching down, he took both my hands in his, speaking softly. "I'm going to be here a while. I want you to wait for me at the Ladysmith Police Station. Detective Ncgobe will drive you there."

Detective Ncgobe, standing behind him, nodded slightly but kept her distance giving us space.

His voice grew softer, "Everything's going to be okay. I wouldn't let anyone hurt you."

He pushed a strand of my hair gently behind my ear. He got up swiftly, striding away before I could find something to say.

Watching Terry go, I was thinking Jay had said the same thing. Where was he and was he okay?

* * *

Detective Ncgobe led me to her unmarked Jetta with a smile. She was very kind as we drove, not saying much until my thoughts of Jay lying unconscious on the floor at Rooikat Cottage had me furiously blinking away tears.

"It's alright, sweetie." Her voice was rich and soothing. "Inspector Grierson won't let those men harm you. He's got quite a reputation for not allowing the bad guys to do anyone harm. In fact, some criminals say he's some kind of devil!" A brilliant grin accompanied that little snippet.

I tried to stop sniffing, liking her more and more. "It's not that," I blubbered.

She offered me some tissues. I accepted gratefully.

I blew my nose before speaking again. "It's my friend. I'm worried about him," I mumbled, then blew again.

"Eish," she sympathised. Then, "You look like you've been through hell. Getting shot at is not much fun, but it's a chance you take if you're with a cop. And your man Grierson is one of the best in the world, they say. So, put your faith in him and in God. You'll never quite get used to the fact he might never return from a day at work, but you can make the best of the time you'll have together. That's what my husband says. It works for me!" She smiled her kind smile again.

I stared at her open-mouthed, struck by the absurdity and sense of *deja vu*. Hadn't I had a similar conversation recently?

"You just see. And if you need to talk..."

"But Grierson's not my boyfriend!"

She looked at me with a 'you're kidding' expression.

I had to set the record straight. "We've only just met! He's actually chased me all the way from Grahamstown and hurt my friend, Jay."

She laughed. "But honey, he's in love with you! It's so obvious from the way he behaves around you. I know. I've seen it a hundred times. You just let him take care of you. He's a good cop. And, it seems he has money, too, from the looks of that car of his. And, ooh, he's a handsome one! It's not just the girls that have been drooling over him!" There was a naughty sparkle in her eyes.

"But..." I remembered where and when I'd had this all too familiar conversation. "It's not like that." My protest sounded as lame as it had before. It was obvious she didn't believe me, just as Patty hadn't believed Jay and I were merely good friends. I was struck by the fact that my life was a whole lot more complicated than even I'd suspected.

* * *

Detective Ncgobe sat me down at the empty staff canteen with a reassuring, "You just wait here, Ms Gonzales. I'm sure the inspector won't be long now. Would you like some tea or coffee?"

"Erm...Coffee, please."

She smiled a goodbye. Going up to the curious old lady behind the counter, she spoke quietly before leaving. The old lady made the coffee quickly then brought it over herself to the long Formica table where I was seated.

"*Daarsy*," she said in a cracked Cape accent, setting the milky, almost overflowing mug down in front of me. She gave me a long assessing look, like a fussy grandmother. "*Jy moet* eat. A nice ham and *tomatie toastie*, né?"

"Oh, no thank you." I smiled. My stomach growled, choosing to fill in the silence, saying otherwise. I had no money on me...

An irritated sound accompanied her suddenly fierce expression. "*Ai man*, don't be stupid! Patricia said to get you anything you like. *En ek wil*, even if she said *nee! Nou*, a ham and *tamatie toastie* of a cheese and *tomatie toastie*?"

"Erm...Ham and tomato." My voice wobbled a little, overwhelmed by all the kindness I was receiving.

Nodding and smiling her approval, she bustled off to the kitchen leaving me to the empty room. Sighing, I took out my cellphone. I needed to call Jay and Mary.

~ 8 ~

NICE GUY

I stared at my trusty old Nokia wondering if it actually was how Terry and Henry had both tracked me down. I frowned, trying to recall a half-remembered article on a woman who'd been stalked by her ex who knew her every move. Deciding it would make no difference if Henry knew my present location or not, I called Jay. He answered on the first ring.

"Sammi! You okay?"

"Jay! I'm fine. Are you? I'm so sorry. I tried to stay, but Grierson—"

"It's okay. I'm fine." I'd never heard him sound so flat before. "Where are you? Ladysmith?"

"*Ja.* At the police station. Henry tried to run us off the road, then some men tried to shoot us."

The silence in response was interspersed by static. That storm was still out there.

"I'll be there in half an hour," said Jay, still sounding flat. "Just wait for me, okay?"

"Sure," I replied automatically, wondering how come all guys used the same tone and phrases with me.

I tried calling Mary. It went directly to voicemail. I left a brief message after her bright greetings, telling her my whereabouts and that everything was fine. My toast arrived soon after, accompanied by another sweet cup of milky coffee. I thanked the lady, blew on the hot bread and took a bite gingerly. It was the most delicious toast I'd ever had—hot and juicy, the smell alone extremely satisfying, with just a hint of herbs. She watched as I chewed and swallowed.

"*Dis baie lekker!*" I said in my best Afrikaans, my accent as atrocious as ever.

She beamed a pleased, gap-toothed smile at me, nodded acknowledgement then bustled off again. I settled down in contentment to enjoy the sandwich. Mary called before I was quite done.

"Sammi? Sorry, I was with a client. Are you alright? What's happened?"

I told her briefly all that had happened since Clarens.

"But that's terrible! How could that man drag you into all these shootings and things! You should sue!"

"Yes," I agreed, not very convincingly.

She picked up on it immediately. "Just what aren't you telling me, Sammi?"

I thought for a moment, how best to tell her...If any of it even made sense...

"Spit it out, Sammi!"

"Okay! Okay It's Grierson. Some people here think he's my boyfriend."

Her response shook me. "Well, it's about time! Not quite the man I'd have chosen for you, but he's very handsome and...interesting."

"Mary! Have you even met him?"

"Yes. He called on us, Vusi and me, to thank us for trying to help his brother. He believes we helped give him a few minutes more with his brother. So how do you feel about him?"

I thought a minute. "Conflicted." That summed it all up nicely.

Mary didn't think so. "So you like him, but..."

"He's quite violent! And arrogant...and..."

"And sexy, and successful, and apparently in love with you," Mary finished for me.

"And I don't trust him," I completed the list.

"But you are attracted to him?"

There was no denying it. "Yes."

Mary sighed. "There are always excuses not to get involved, isn't there, Sammi?"

There was nothing to say. She was right.

"Did you make your wish at the labyrinth?"

"*Ja*. Just before this whole thing blew up."

"Well, don't you think this may be the universe showing you that this is the guy for you—your soul-mate?"

"But he's not husband material! I wished for a husband, not some...some He-man!"

"Well...Maybe you're getting what you need. Not what you think you need," suggested Mary, sounding ever so reasonable.

I sighed. It still didn't sound or feel right to me. "So you think I need a He-man?"

"All I'm suggesting, Sammi, is that you give this guy a chance."

I sighed again, my heart feeling odd, like my tummy when I was nervous. "Alright. I'll think about it."

"Good." Mary's relief carried clearly. "You holding up okay?"

"Just about. Most people are being incredibly kind."

"Good. So you'll keep me posted."

"*Ja*. Catch you later."

"Bye now."

I looked at my cellphone again. It stared back as innocently as ever, then winked at me as the key-lock activated and went blank-faced. I went over to the lady behind the counter.

"Sorry, but do you have a pen and some paper?"

"Of course!" She tore off some pages of what looked like an order pad and handed them over with a yellow BIC.

"*Dankie!*" I smiled. She smiled back and went back to her baking.

I sat down at the table and carefully wrote down all my contact numbers. I'd never been any good at remembering them. Then I tucked away the pages, deleted most of the numbers, returned the pen, and placed my cellphone carefully on the table, reminding myself to leave it behind when I left.

Terry arrived after what seemed an eternity. He smiled when he saw me, his face instantly changing from stern to charming. "They're taking good care of you?"

I nodded and smiled briefly. I'd had time enough to decide the direct approach would be best. "Jay's on his way to fetch me. I'll leave my phone with you so there's no need for me to hang around."

At the first mention of Jay, Terry's expression had frozen. Disappointment, and something else I couldn't quite identify, flickered across his face before it settled back into inscrutability as I ended.

"You're right," he agreed easily. "I've no right to have put you in such danger, nor to keep you here. When's Jay arriving?"

"He should be here any minute now." I tried to hide my surprise at his easy acceptance of our plan. It didn't quite add up to the rest of what I knew of him.

"Great! This your phone?"

I nodded.

"Thanks. I'll return it when I'm done. You know I really appreciate all your help. You've been a star."

I didn't say anything, just watched as he pocketed my phone and sat on the edge of the table, one leg swinging free.

"It's been quite an adventure for you, hasn't it?" he laughed, turning it all into a joke.

I didn't mind, sick of all the tension. "Yes, it has." I smiled again, "I won't forget it for a long time."

"I hope you won't forget me either!"

"How could I?" I leant my elbows on the table, not far from his knee. "What will you do once you've caught Henry?"

"You seem sure I will?"

"*Ja.* Call me psychic!"

He gave that easy laugh again, but his look was intense. His eyes dropped suddenly. "I was thinking of quitting all of this...Trying something new."

"Like what? Farming?"

He shook his head. "No. That was Lionel's thing. I've never had the patience for farming. Security consulting or project management, perhaps...Or maybe I'll finally get round to practising Environmental Law."

"That might be good. It sounds less dangerous than running after criminals. And you still get to nail them. Unless you decide to defend them."

"Never!"

"Cool." I spotted the unmistakable figure of Jay striding towards the canteen. "Jay's here!"

Terry stood up, asking casually, "Do you think he'll mind giving me a lift to Durban?"

I remembered Jay's flat tone. Together with the expression on his approaching face, I thought the most likely answer would be no. "Eerm.."

"It's alright. I understand." Terry was still being Mr Nice Guy.

"Understand what?" greeted Jay sharply.

"Hi Jay. Terry was just wondering if you'd give him a lift to Durban."

Jay looked at him incredulously.

"Well, I assumed you're heading in that direction, and if it's no bother..."

Jay's eyes bounced from Terry to me and back again, still with that incredulous look.

"It will help me catch Henry that much faster," added Terry at his most persuasive.

Jay finally spoke. "Sammi, could I have a word with you." Then to Terry, "Do you mind?"

"Sure," went Terry, walking away towards the far end of the room.

***

Jay spoke in an undertone. "What the hell is he up to?"

"He wants to catch Henry."

"By putting you in danger again?"

"I shouldn't be in any danger."

"How did they trace you then? Cellphone?"

"That's what Terry thinks."

"Where's it now?"

I jerked my head towards Terry, "I gave it to him to help catch Henry."

Jay nodded his head slowly. "So he can let Henry trace him via your phone. Why does he want to come with us? Can't he requisition a car? What happened to his?"

"Tyres shot out. Windscreen's gone."

Jay looked agitated. "Let me get this straight. He wants to get a lift with us to Durbs, despite being in a police station in a large town with many other options."

I nodded uncomfortably.

"He's also got your cellphone," continued Jay, "through which he hopes to make direct contact with Henry—a man who's tried to kill you about four times now."

I was dumbstruck. Had it really been four times?

"Don't you think you're pushing your luck, Sammi? And that Grierson's asking too much of you? I'd never put you in such danger."

Before I could think of anything to say, he'd strode over to Terry.

"I'm sorry, Inspector. We can't help you."

Terry nodded, ignoring Jay's almost rude tone, dismissive of him as he walked back to me. Then he checked himself. "Jay, this is my phone number. Call me if you run into Henry. And could I have your phone number, too?"

Jay looked at him blankly, then took the pre-offered card. "Why'd you need my number?"

"In case we need to clarify some things with Samantha."

Jay gave him a suspicious look, but recited his number anyway.

"Thanks, mate," said Terry, ever the nice guy. He made to clap Jay on the shoulder, but Jay stepped smartly out of range. He nodded at him instead. Terry took my hands, shaking them warmly in both of his large ones. His smile was brilliant as he said, "Call me if I can help with anything. Anything at all."

He held my hands for a few moments longer than necessary, looking deep into my eyes with his amazing green ones, then abruptly strode briskly away.

Jay was looking on, standing with his feet wide apart, arms crossed, an unfriendly look on his face. "What the hell was all that about?"

~ 9 ~

THE N3

Jay absentmindedly held the Mini's door for me, lost in dark thoughts. I got in. He stood for a few seconds, only his torso visible to me. I thought he was gazing at the station entrance. Then he strode around the little car and got in, a slight frown on his face. He didn't look at me or say anything, just got us back onto the main road, Stereophonics playing on the sound-system. The melancholy, whimsical sound perfectly matched our moods. Jay broke the silence a few minutes down the N3.

"So what happened after he knocked me out?"

"He chased Henry, dragging me along because he thought at first that I was in league with Henry."

"So what changed his mind?"

"I hadn't tried to help Henry. He said...," I paused, trying to remember exactly how Terry had phrased it.

"He said what?"

"Basically, he said that he could see I wasn't a criminal."

"So he chased Henry, but didn't catch him?"

"No. It was terrifying! We went speeding down Golden Gate after him. Henry managed to get behind us and rammed us, trying to make us crash. We didn't—only just—but he got away."

"And you and Grierson bonded."

"I wouldn't exactly put it that way!"

"Oh?" It was almost accusatory.

I wondered why I was feeling so defensive. "We started to chat...And got to know each other a little."

Jay was staring fixedly ahead. "And now you like him."

"*Jaaa*...He's a nice guy when you get to know him."

Jay seemed to tense, squeezing the steering wheel, then relaxing again. "Who shot at you?"

"I don't know. There was this *bakkie*. They shot out the tyres and the windscreen. Terry managed to get us onto the shoulder. We ran into the bush. Two of them followed us. Terry fought the one. Kicked this anthill into his face—"

Jay smiled grimly.

"Then we ran again, Terry taking the man's gun. He left me in hiding then went back to deal with the other guy. He ended up shooting the guy. The *bakkie* driver came back. He had a pistol and a bush-knife. Terry jumped him and disarmed him. Then the police and everybody else came."

"A dangerous man, our Mr Grierson." remarked Jay.

"Yes. You shouldn't have rushed at him like that."

Jay's smile was rueful. "*Ja*, I shouldn't have rushed him. My mistake," he ended softly.

I glanced at him sharply. I didn't think Jay had been agreeing with me. "Jay, you mustn't fight with him, okay?" I pleaded in concern.

"Afraid I'll hurt him?"

"No, I'm afraid he'll hurt *you* again. I don't ever want to see that again, either."

Jay laughed his old laugh, brightening up the car's atmosphere immediately. "You won't!" he promised with a smile.

I knew that smile. It did nothing to reassure me.

"That whole shooting seems much more than just a normal hijacking."

I agreed.

"Do they think Henry set it up?"

"I don't know. They didn't tell me anything."

"Not even your friend, Terry?"

"No, we didn't talk that much since the shooting."

"Hmm...Did he mention what all this is about? It would be nice to know why you're being shot at."

"No. Terry didn't tell me anything. Just that this is part of a bigger investigation. And he wants to get Henry for killing his brother." Through the window, I watched the mountains roll by. The Berg was brooding under some dark cloud. It looked like it might snow.

"I've been doing some digging of my own. A friend of mine told me the bank password is for an account that holds £20 million. It's held by a company called WC Consultants. He's finding out more about the company for me."

"Shew! That explains a lot. Twenty million Pounds!" It was almost an inconceivable amount to me. I remembered something Terry had mentioned. "Is this your hacker friend, Ha ser Ren?"

He looked at me in surprise. "Ha Sibh Ken. Who told you about him? Grierson?"

"*Ja.* He said he thinks you helped your friend hack into some government sites and shifted money around."

"Did he now?"

"*Ja,* he did. It sounded like something we both talked about at Tech. Remember?"

"I remember. Talked to Tom about it, too," was all he admitted.

I decided the air needed clearing. "Terry also told me you broke a man's back in Germany. In some bar. You didn't, did you?"

I watched him try to strangle the steering wheel again, his long, usually elegant fingers whitening. Then the slow relaxation again. His silence was eloquent.

"He said you should have been in jail but pleaded self-defence and won." I spoke softly, hoping he'd confirm my thoughts.

"He said that, did he? You agree with him?"

"Jay," I began gently, "I know you. You don't get into bar fights. You don't hurt people if you can help it. And you don't lie. I don't believe you'd have pleaded self-defence if it wasn't."

He kept his silence, his thoughts far away.

I realised how hard this was for him. My prying wasn't fair. "You don't have to tell me if you don't want to. Oh, look! The sluices are open!" I was hoping to change the subject by pointing out one of his favourite sights on the road—the open sluices at Wagondrift Dam.

The distraction didn't work. He sighed wearily. "I wanted to tell you, but couldn't. And every time I tried, there was always something else going on. So, I never quite got to it."

"Jay, you don't have to—"

"But I want to. I've wanted to for the longest time. I need to..."

He took a moment to gather his thoughts as I watched the Estcourt hills roll by, starting to turn brown.

* * *

Eventually, he said, "I was hanging out with a bunch of guys who were backpacking like me. Tom, another Scot called Grant, a couple of Aussies, two English guys—Jerry and David, and Ben, and Pal. Ben's French and Pal's Norwegian. I've only kept in touch with Tom, Ben and Pal since. The others weren't really great company. But they were friends of Tom. We did Spain, Portugal, The Netherlands and Germany together. We thought we were so cool. Did some crazy things, lots of parties. They drank a lot. You know the sort of crowd I mean."

I nodded. They weren't his sort of crowd at all considering his boredom threshold was even lower than mine, especially when it came to drunken chatter.

"So anyway, we got to Germany, which seemed to be one big party back then. Most of the guys ended up pretty much out of it most of the time. Tom and I would see them all safely back. To be honest, I was getting sick of it all." He paused again. Good Charlotte began to play. "I told the guys I was leaving for Norway and naturally it was another excuse for a huge binge. We ended up going with these girls to a new bar. It was very Skinhead. Neo-Nazi types proudly showing off their tattoos... I'm not sure how it all began, but these two Skinheads started laying into Ben. Tom and I went over to try to stop them. They pulled out knives. It all turned ugly before we quite knew it. The whole bar was fighting by then, broken bottles, flying chairs...It was incredibly scary.

"The two Skinheads were trying to knife Ben and Tom, who'd got to them before me. Ben was already cut on his arm and Tom was trying his best not to be stabbed. I know I was yelling at them to stop. I helped get the one guy off Tom, but his friend came for me with that knife...Next thing I know, the guy is laying across a chair-back screaming. Seems I'd thrown him onto it."

I shivered, staring wide-eyed at Jay, remembering Mike's screams when he'd broken his arm back at Tech.

He glanced at me, then smiled sardonically. "Not one of my finest moments." And then he fell silent, waiting for me to say something.

I wondered how best to put it. "It was self-defence, Jay. If anybody came at me with a knife, I'd probably try my best to stop them...somehow. I mean, I even thought of smashing a lamp on Henry's head not six hours ago!"

He smiled slowly. Then, "I can just see it!" he chuckled.

I thought again about Mike's broken arm. "Well now that we are discussing our violent tendencies, I've always wondered why you beat Mike Labuschagne up. What did he do, or say?" I sensed Jay starting to shut down again. "Jay?"

He sighed once again. "Mike was a pig."

I waited for him to elaborate.

"I was....defending a girl's honour. He said some hateful things about her and... Let's just leave it at that, okay?"

"Okay. Was it Rachel?" I couldn't help but ask. Jay had seemed sweet on her back then.

"No."

I gave him a curious glance. That was a you've-hit-a-stone-wall no. I left it at that.

We were a couple of kilometres from the Shell Rest-stop when Jay asked, "Need to stop?"

"No, I'm fine."

"How's your side?"

I'd almost forgotten about it. "Fine." I reassured him. We passed the stop. It looked packed. I could imagine the queues.

"So, you know my deepest darkest secret now. Time for you to tell all," suggested Jay.

I looked at him again, doubting that was indeed his deepest, darkest secret. Jay often had a way of being more than enigmatic.

"Come on, Sammi. Spit it out!"

"Don't have one."

"Everybody has one."

"Not me."

Jay shot me a disappointed look. "There must be something...Come on, Sammi, give!"

"Oh, alright! I'll make one up!"

Jay smiled. "Nah, it's got to be a real one."

I sighed. I couldn't think of anything that came even close to being a deep, dark secret.

"Okay, okay! I don't have a deep, dark secret, but I do have a secret, sort of."

"I'm all ears."

"Great, flapping ears."

He grinned hugely.

"Well, I wasn't just meditating at the labyrinth, I was making a wish...For a husband...and a child. I've always wanted to be a mother." I ended wistfully.

He glanced at me. "I know," he said simply.

"Really?" I didn't remember talking to him about it recently. Only Mary knew how important this was to me. "Anyway," I went on, wanting to get his opinion. "Mary thinks me meeting Terry is a sign from the universe that he's the one for me."

"Bullshit!" was Jay's prompt response, which had been close to my initial reaction, but I wanted to hear what else he thought. He went on. "If that were true, taking into account that the universe almost killed you in the process—thrice—then it could just as well have been Henry who's the one for you—or me!"

I looked at him amused. He seemed remarkably serious. Annoyed even.

"You sweet on him?" He glared at me.

I giggled, then matched his tone. "But Mary's not been wrong about my life so far."

"She's your psychic?"

"And friend and teacher," I clarified.

"You gonna let you tell her how to live your life?"

"No. Her readings are just a tool—like a weather report."

He glanced at me doubtfully. "Then don't believe all she tells you. She may only be seeing part of it."

"How would you know?"

"Trust me."

"I do. I just want to know how you know about psychics. Have you been to one?"

"No,"

He was being evasive again. *Why?* "Jay?"

"Sammi, that wasn't a good secret. Almost everyone knows about it. You'll have to tell me another one."

"Who's everyone?" I hadn't been aware my deepest wish was so well known.

"Your parents, your sister, me and Mary, it seems. Now quit stalling. I want to hear a *real* secret!"

I looked in resignation at the steadily winding road, enjoying the way the car sat firmly on the bends, and how smoothly Jay drove.

"I'm waiting," Jay tried a Darth Vader voice. He'd never been very good at it.

I knew I had to tell him something, though. He was being at his most tenacious. It was unlikely he'd let this go. "My deepest secret... is..." I stalled, not sure if I was ashamed or just incredibly shy about the whole thing. It was so personal, so intimate.

"Hmm?" encouraged Jay.

"I'm a virgin." I got it out as fast as I could.

Jay was changing down. He ground the gears.

I felt the flush on my face grow. I didn't dare look at him. I'd never told anyone else this, just letting them assume whatever they wished. After all, it was nobody else's business.

"For sure," said Jay carefully. "I did wonder..."

"Wonder what?"

He started to say something, then changed it to, "I think it's great! You're waiting for the right man—the man who'll be your husband, right? It's great. Really special. It shows..."

"Shows what?" My tone sounded defensive, even to me.

"It shows an endearing faithfulness. And makes your commitment, when you do eventually make it, remarkably special...and precious...I think..."

I thought about it for a minute, wondering if he truly believed it or was just trying to make me feel better.

"Jay, I'm thirty-three years old. It's not normal for someone my age to still be a virgin!"

"You know everyone's sexual history, do you?"

"No."

"Then how could you possibly know what is normal? Lots of people lie about sex. It's a natural pastime. There's probably lots more people like you—virgins in their thirties and forties—some of whom might remain virgins all their lives. There's nothing wrong with it."

"You mean like nuns."

He smiled. "Actually, I don't think all nuns are virgins."

"Jay!"

He grinned, "Well some of them take their vows in their late twenties, don't they?"

I didn't know much about nuns so I left it at that. But I was more curious than ever. "Are you a virgin?"

"No."

"Did you sleep with a lot of girls, then?"

"No. A couple."

"A couple or a few?"

"A couple."

"At the same time!"

"No!" He laughed with a blush. "You were always more naughty than you looked!" he accused playfully.

I giggled again, as we slalomed down the N3 easily. Jay started to sing. I joined in, trying to sing along to the 'Nudies' 'Managing Mula'. I settled back into the comfortable seat, feeling at peace and relaxed after what seemed like a lifetime, glad I'd never have to see Henry, nor experience the violence that accompanied him, ever again.

* * *

Jay was in the middle of telling me a hysterically funny story about his friend Tom when his phone rang.

"Could you get that?"

"Sure."

I answered the call, "Jay's phone. May I help you?" in my best Moneypenny accent.

"Samantha!" It was Terry.

"Hi!" I squealed in surprise, vaguely pleased. I hadn't expected to hear from him this soon, if ever.

"Samantha, can you talk?" His voice didn't sound as pleased as mine. It was stern and tense—the old Grierson.

I sobered up immediately. "What is it?"

Jay shot me a quizzical look. 'Terry' I mouthed back as Terry started to speak.

"I wish I didn't have to ask but we—I—need your help."

"Yes?" I encouraged, not liking the sound of it at all.

"Look, first of all, where are you?"

My sense of dread grew. Jay shot me another questioning look: *What does he want?* I shrugged, and answered Terry. "We're in the Midlands. We passed Mooi River Toll about ten minutes ago."

"Good. I can meet you at Granny Mouse's. Have lunch. It's on me. I'm about forty-five minutes to an hour behind you."

"Terry, what's this all about?" I was clutching the phone tightly.

Jay was beginning to frown.

"I'll explain when I see you."

"But, Terry—"

"Later." he said, cutting the call.

"What'd he want?" demanded Jay in concern.

"To meet us at Granny Mouse's in about an hour. He said to have lunch on him."

"Why?"

"He said he'll explain when he sees us."

Jay snorted in disgust. "I don't feel like stopping at Granny Mouse's. Do you?"

"I've never been to Granny Mouse's," I replied, images of Sunday cartoon mice in my mind. "But I don't particularly want to have a big lunch. I just want to get home and rest."

Jay nodded. "That's settled then. We'll push on. He can tell you what he wants over the phone."

"Great. I'll just tell call him to let him know..." Jay gave me a stubborn look in return. "Jay!"

He relented, grudgingly, "Okay, then. But if I were you, I'd make him wait."

"Don't be silly!" I scrolled over to the call list and dialled Terry's number.

Terry was not pleased. "Jay put you up to this," he growled.

"No, I'm the one who wants to get home quickly," I defended Jay. "What's all this about, then?"

He took a moment to answer. "It's Henry."

My heart began to race as fear gripped me. I was clenching the phone so hard my hand was hurting. "Did you find him?" My voice was sharp with dread.

"No, but he found me via your cellphone. And he knows where you are right now."

I couldn't breathe. "How?" I whispered. It shouldn't have been possible. Jay was indicating and slowing down, pulling over onto the shoulder.

"I don't know, Samantha. Maybe he truly is psychic! The point is: you're still in danger and Henry still seems to have the advantage."

Jay stopped the car, hazards blinking, and gently took the phone from my suddenly nerveless hands.

"Grierson."

Terry's voice came to me as a muted rumble sounding much less friendly.

Jay listened, staring intently into the distance, checking the rear-view and side-mirrors occasionally. "Hmm. Is there another way?"

Terry's answer was brief.

"I'm not bringing Sammi to you just so you can send her into danger again." Jay was intractable once more.

Terry rumbled in response. I knew he was giving Jay an ultimatum from the way Jay's eyes narrowed and his face went blank.

"'K," was all Jay said, cutting the call with Terry still rumbling what I took to be more threats. Cancelling the hazards, Jay merged us into the light traffic, his face set.

"What did he say?"

"He said the best chance we have of keeping you alive and out of Henry's clutches is to co-operate with him." He paused. "He also said he'd throw me in jail for obstructing justice and attacking a police officer if I don't have you at Granny Mouse's in an hour."

"I'm sorry, Jay."

"It's not your fault."

I wondered why Terry was being so mean to Jay when being nice produced much better results. Why hadn't Terry kept the same attitude he'd had at the police station? I shook my head in confusion. Guys were so irrational. I couldn't figure them out at all. Jay didn't say anything more, just concentrated on his driving and on finding the right off-ramp. We reached Granny Mouse's twenty minutes later in the driving rain.

~ 10 ~

GRANNY MOUSE'S

The restaurant was cosy, made to look like a farmhouse kitchen. Jay took a cursory look at the menu. "Beef Fillet," he ordered.

I chose the lamb. We both asked for Earl Grey tea. The waitress took the menu away with a smile. We stared at each other. Jay's eyes were dark and shiny, tiny water droplets stuck to his long eyelashes, his hair sticking up like a porcupine. He was still furious. I caught my reflection in a mirror. I looked like the ghost of a drowned rat spooked by itself—all pale with soaking flat hair and wide eyes.

"I should have ordered the Lobster Thermidor," remarked Jay eventually.

I laughed. "And I, the salmon."

"It's not too late."

I wondered if he meant changing the order or getting back into the Mini and driving off. So far, Jay had proven the safest option for me, always making the best choices.

He smiled conspiratorially, reading my mind. "Change places with me," he suggested.

I complied, wondering why he wanted a view out the window. The answer struck me almost immediately—to see Terry drive up. What was Jay up to? Our teas arrived, an oasis of fragrant civilization in a less than civilised 72 hours. I closed my eyes, inhaling the steam deeply, letting it relax me and help the circulation in my face.

"You wearing mascara, or did your eyelashes get thicker?" asked Jay.

"What?" I looked up to see if he was teasing me. It was impossible to tell. He wore his serious scientist face, one he also wore to take the mickey out of people.

"Your eyelashes. They're thicker than before. I'd swear it. Are you wearing mascara?"

I half laughed. "When would I've had the time?"

He continued to study my face, tea apparently forgotten. It was disconcerting. I blushed and looked into the black depths of my tea as if there might be some answer to a vital question there. But there were no tea-leaves in this cup. I contemplated breaking the teabag in the pot.

"No, they're definitely thicker than I remember. They make your eyes seem larger."

"Well, they aren't as long and thick as yours. Any camel would be proud to have yours. But I think they look much better on you than they would on any camel." I added.

He looked down at me, somehow contriving to peep through those very same eyelashes. His eyes had lightened, his anger forgotten or simmering much further down.

His smile was bashful. "Why, thank you ma'am," he drawled in a ridiculously fake Texan accent. "I do believe that was a fair good compliment."

"Oh, stop fishing!" I mock-scolded with a grin.

His expression suddenly changed.

Alarmed, I leant forward in concern, "What?"

"I really want some of that salmon," he explained, turning around to search for the waitress. She was at our table before he could even raise his hand. "Could we have some of that salmon, please?"

"Certainly, sir." She gave him a brilliant smile before heading off to the kitchen.

I lifted my eyebrows. "Looks like you have an admirer there."

He turned to watch her shapely retreating figure. "Perhaps she likes a man with good taste," he mused.

"Or," I grinned at him, "She might like camels!"

He laughed. One of my favourite sounds.

* * *

Terry arrived in a white unmarked Opel Astra just as Jay and I were almost done with our delicious feast. There was no sign of the salmon, with a third of the Beef Fillet headed for the doggie bag. Terry parked the Astra right in front of the window, turning it towards the drive before stepping out. He spotted us immediately, nodded, and headed for the entrance.

"Jay!" I warned, afraid he might do something that would get him hurt again, images of Terry's devastating fighting techniques springing into my mind. Jay just smiled benignly, clasping my hand in reassurance.

Terry walked in, his gaze instantly falling on Jay's hand on mine. Jay gave me a gently comforting squeeze, then let go.

"Hello, Inspector," greeted Jay, playing it cool.

Terry gave him a suspicious look, then nodded, pulling up a chair to sit down next to me. Jay did his magic on the waitress.

"Coffee," ordered Terry, sending her back into the kitchen before she could throw Jay another smile.

She threw one at Terry instead. Jay grinned at me. I smiled back.

Terry cleared his throat. "I'm glad you decided to help, Samantha," he began.

"It's not like we had much of a choice," murmured Jay.

Terry ignored him, concentrating on me. He took my hand in his. "I know how difficult this must be for you."

"So how does Henry keep finding her? What does he want now?" Jay's tone was businesslike—reasonable, but insistent. Terry couldn't ignore it without looking churlish.

He turned to face Jay, face growing stern again, "We don't know. We thought he tracked her through her cell. He did call it, but asked to speak to me. We think now that he has inside help from someone on the case—or someone close to Sammi." The last was said with a meaningful look at Jay.

Jay's eyes grew wide, "Who? You?"

Terry smiled darkly. "The general thinking is you, given your previous record."

"Of being her friend for over fifteen years," finished Jay, still with mock disbelief.

"People change," Terry ground out, daggers in his eyes.

"Like cops who start being criminals?" suggested Jay equably.

I sat in the middle, open-mouthed as the guys locked-eyes like two bulls locking horns.

"That's grounds for slander," growled Terry.

"Just what I was thinking," smiled Jay, eyes glittering dangerously.

I retrieved my hand from Terry's. "Guys, could we just remain focussed here. Henry still thinks I have that list of numbers, doesn't he?"

"Don't you?" Terry seemed surprised.

Jay stared at him, answering for me, "No, she doesn't."

Terry ignored him once more. "Do you have it or not, Samantha?"

His green eyes bore into mine making me feel nervous. "No, I gave it to Jay."

He glared at Jay. "Why?"

"Safe-keeping," supplied Jay. I opened my mouth to object, but Jay's slight movement of his fingers checked me.

"Give it to me!" demanded Terry, his full attention on Jay now.

I was back to not liking him. You'd have thought he'd have realised by now that intimidation and rudeness didn't endear him to anybody, least of all to Jay.

"Certainly," agreed Jay, unexpectedly.

"Now!"

"It's in my other pants pocket. In the Mini. I'll just go get it." Terry was still glaring as Jay got up leisurely and stretched. "Won't be a minute," smiled Jay.

His phone rang. Excusing himself to the other diners, he left the restaurant.

* * *

Terry tried to take my hand again, but I didn't want him to. I used it to brush my hair off my face. "Now what?" I was surprised at how tired and resigned my voice sounded. "Will Henry leave me alone now that he'll get those numbers?"

Terry put his hand on my arm instead. "I'm sorry Samantha. It's not as easy as that. Henry wants you to hand over the numbers to him yourself—alone."

I stared at him in disbelief, his hand feeling heavy and uncomfortable on my arm. "You're kidding, right!" I tried to shrug off his hand, but it remained immovable. He shook his head. "But why?" I tried not to whinge. "What could he possibly want with me?"

"You're still the only witness to Lionel's death. Without you, the case against Henry could fall apart." His eyes fell. "I'm sorry Samantha. I have to take you into protective custody again, and try to find a way to get Henry when he comes for those numbers, and for you." He looked at me again. "I truly wish there was another way."

I could only stare at him, dumbfounded.

"I'll keep you safe," he promised.

"How can you?" I croaked, close to tears. "You can't stop him from tracking me. And you won't even be able to stop him from shooting me again!"

"Samantha," he said gently, squeezing my arm once more.

I couldn't stand it any more. Couldn't stand to look at his pleading face or have him touching me. I shot up from my chair, and ran blindly out of the restaurant, craving only fresh air and escape.

Outside, it was raining softly once more. Cool, large raindrops fell down on my face, merging with my tears. I was aware of Terry entering the large covered patio, stopping near the door to watch me. Jay ambled over in his old hoodie, a bright red parka over his arm. He threw it over me and steered me towards an old oak tree. That brought Terry swiftly to my other side, trying to steer me back to the patio.

"Just stop it!" I yelled, throwing them both off and running towards the little garaged area where the Mini was parked. I sank down against it, sobbing. I wasn't going back with Terry to face Henry. I'd keep on running—even if it had to be for my whole life!

* * *

I stood squarely facing Terry five minutes later. "I want Jay to come with me." I tried to keep my tone as flat as possible to avoid a sob escaping.

He crossed his arms and widened his stance, trying to soften the hard expression that instantly arose at my statement. My false courage began to desert me.

"No." Terry's tone was uncompromising.

Behind me, Jay stepped closer, not quite touching my back. He seemed relaxed, offering support and comfort if I needed it. I couldn't see him but I knew he had his arms in his pockets, head cocked to one side, shoulders hunched, watching Terry with subdued curiosity.

"I won't come otherwise," I stated. It came out louder than I meant, despite my constricted throat. Terry's expression didn't change. "You can't make me," I added, with conviction, suddenly understanding that he couldn't.

Terry sighed. "Samantha," the voice of reason once again, persuasive. "He's not trained for dealing with such situations. He'll get you both killed. Are you sure you want to place him in such danger?"

I turned to face Jay, uncertainty rearing its head once more. I hadn't thought of things in that way.

Terry continued. "I have training and experience, Samantha. I know how to deal with people like Henry. I'll make sure you don't come to any harm."

"What kind of training?" Jay was still all mild curiosity.

"You saw." Terry's glance at him was as terse as his reply.

"Hmm." Jay's tone was merely one of reflection. "Not such a good track record for keeping her safe then."

Terry stepped meaningfully forward, glaring at Jay. Jay didn't move. I was sandwiched between the two of them, outright hostility and calm wariness. Feeling Terry's anger growing, I took a cautionary step back, half expecting to thread on Jay's feet. But I didn't. He'd stepped back with me. A small part of me wondered at that. Terry took another step forward. I pushed out my hands in reflex. "Just stop, okay! I'm not going anywhere without Jay!"

Terry's breath heaved through his nostrils, his eyes glittered. He took a deep breath, inflating his broad chest even more. I could feel Jay's amusement. *Alpha male peacock* came unbidden into my mind. I frowned slightly. *Where had that thought come from?*

Terry conceded. "Fine! We'll all go in the Astra. I'll drive."

His face darkened as Jay said, "No way I'm leaving the Mini."

"Then you'll follow us."

"Not likely, Inspector. There's no telling what you'll do to throw me off. You can follow us."

I could see things beginning to slide back to square one. *Men!* "I want to go in the Mini. And it's less conspicuous than the police car," I declared, feeling like an underpaid schoolmarm.

Terry looked down at me in disappointment. But I was right. And they both knew it.

"Fine," Terry repeated. "But I'm coming with you so *he*," jerking his head at Jay, "doesn't try to give me the slip."

We both looked at Jay, who still looked slightly amused. He nodded slowly.

"Fair enough."

* * *

The Mini felt cramped with Terry's dominating presence. The current tension was in marked contrast to the earlier camaraderie Jay and I had shared. I was in the backseat, being the shortest.

I'd chosen it, noticing the diabolical grin on Jay's face when he'd opened the car door. Before he could suggest Terry squeeze into the back, I'd slipped in and settled myself comfortably, saying a short nap would do me good. With both of them being almost the same height, there wasn't much space to put my feet down, so I made a bit of a nest for myself by piling the bags on one side of the seat and piling the coats and jerseys on the other side to make a pillow of sorts. Then I curled up as best I could, slumping against the back-rest, seatbelt on as usual. I never went in a car without wearing a seatbelt, ever.

Jay glanced at me as he turned back to reverse the car. He grinned. "Comfortable?"

I nodded with a smile.

Jay drove easily up the muddy drive to the main road.

"Where to?" he asked Terry, who'd been quiet and thoughtful since he'd gotten into the Mini and Jay had handed him those numbers.

"Midlands Mall."

Jay shrugged, and headed for the N3. "So how's this going to work?"

Terry stared straight ahead. I thought at first he wasn't going to answer.

Finally, he said, "Henry wants to rendezvous at the Mall. He wants Samantha to meet him, alone, with the numbers."

"Then what?"

"He said he needs to talk to her. Not hurt her. Once he's spoken to her and has the numbers, he'll leave her alone."

"That doesn't make sense. It sounds like a trade-off. But, Henry's got nothing to trade, has he?"

"He's got information I need. And he's got his life."

"His life? For what?"

"Samantha's."

Jay looked sharply at Terry, who sat impassively, still looking directly ahead.

I sat up straighter. "But..."

Jay got there quicker, "What aren't you telling us, Grierson?"

"Police business," was the terse reply.

Jay was thoughtful at that.

"How are you going to make sure Henry doesn't just shoot me, Terry?" My concern had me leaning forward, hanging onto Terry's seat. "After all, he's such a good liar and actor. He had us all convinced at the weekend. And I'll still be a threat to him, even if you get him this time."

Terry twisted round to face me. "We'll have undercover police all around the area. I'll have you and Henry in my sight at all times."

"Do you think that will be enough, Grierson." Jay didn't sound satisfied at that news at all. "He's proved himself to be audacious and ruthless. How do you know he won't just shoot Sammi and run off again."

"I'll shoot him myself, if he does. He knows I'll have my sights on him the entire time. I've told him so already."

Jay still wasn't convinced. "I thought the idea was to prevent Sammi being hurt, not just to get Henry out in the open."

I looked at Terry askance.

He looked me in the eye. "I promise you, Sammi, you won't get hurt again."

I exchanged a look with Jay in the rear-view mirror. We both knew it wasn't a promise Terry could keep.

* * *

I closed my eyes against a growing headache. Tense with worry and stress, I hadn't expected to doze off, but I did. The two guys talked in a low soothing rumble, conversing civilly for a change instead of sniping at each other. Every now and then, I'd catch snatches of the conversation between the songs and the road noises. They seemed to be discussing cars at one point. At another point, I heard Terry saying, "...intend marrying her, that's why." I wondered dozily if he perhaps meant me, then decided not. What might have been a few seconds or minutes later, Jay said, "If you hurt her, I'll make sure..." The Mini went back to feeling safe and cosy. I dreaded having to leave it.

~ 11 ~

MIDLANDS MALL

We reached the mall in the late afternoon. Terry directed Jay to the north side, near the service entrance. Jay pulled into a free space. It was cloudy with a cold wind swaying the trees on the bank in front of us. Terry stepped out the Mini almost as soon as the car stopped. "I'll go speak to the team."

"We'll have some coffee at the Wimpy," Jay told him, getting out too. He stretched leisurely as Terry hurried off to find the police team. "Come on, Sleeping Beauty. We're here," cajoled Jay, peering into the back-seat.

I moved with reluctance.

He leant over the seat. "Hey." His voice was soft. "It's almost over. It's going to be alright. Let's get some coffee. Henry's not likely to try anything in a busy mall. We'll wait for Grierson and his team comfortably."

I gazed at Jay, noticing there were more lines around his eyes than I'd remembered. They looked like laugh lines. He held out his hand and nodded outside. I wondered why I'd always found Jay so convincing. Probably because he'd never let me down and always seemed to be proven right even when I hated the answer. Sighing, I let him help me out of the car and stuck close to him, half hoping he'd put an arm around me. I needed the comfort and warmth. But he didn't, saying instead, "Let's go."

We found a Wimpy at the opposite end of the mall, almost empty at that time of day. It had its own Ladies which I used gratefully. I'd dreaded walking down the long corridors to the public ones with an eye out for Henry and no Jay or Terry by my side. Our order had arrived by the time I got back to our table. As usual, the waitress was trying to flirt with Jay. He was being polite. He smiled as he saw me approaching. She looked at me with envy and left. I smiled in amusement.

"What?"

"Nothing."

"Give!" he demanded.

I smiled again. "It's just that it seems where-ever we go, you're a waitress magnet!"

He laughed. "Just as well. There aren't many waiters about serving us today!"

The coffee was as good as ever. Out of the blue, Jay grabbed my wrist, locking his long fingers around it.

"What? Jay!"

"What do you do to break the hold?" His look was serious.

"Oh, come on, Jay! I don't think—"

"Humour me. How would you break the hold. Pretend I'm Henry?"

His hand was warm, holding my wrist firmly, but not uncomfortably so, just insistent; but I could easily see how it would be painful if he held on just a little bit tighter. I tried to remember the few self-defence lessons I'd taken. My mind remained blank. I attempted to swat his face with my free hand.

He captured that hand, too, in the same lock with a, "That's not gonna work. Try something else."

I curled my fist and tried jerking it to the left, the right, up, down...It was no use. He just shook his head, my two hands still captive.

"Listen carefully," he instructed. "This is what you do. Open your fist. Keep your fingers straight. Turn your wrist as much as you can until your wrist-bone is in line with his thumb. Then slide your hand towards his thumb, moving in an arc. Got it?"

I nodded.

"Good. Now give it a try."

I did as I had been told, frowning in concentration, fighting the urge to curl my fists again. My hand slipped out fairly easily despite Jay's attempts to hold on even harder. I grinned at Jay in pleased amazement.

He grinned back. "Then you hit his nose or claw his eyes. Whatever feels right. Then you run, okay?"

"Okay," I nodded back, feeling much better and confident.

"Great. Now do it again." Jay caught my wrists once more.

We practised breaking the hold a few times.

"There's something else I wanted to show you," Jay remarked, gulping down the remainder of his rapidly cooling coffee.

"Hmm hmm?" I waited with keen interest.

"If you want him to fall, you push him under the chin with the palm of your hand. Don't stop the motion. Push in an arc as far back as your arm stretches. He'll start to loose balance before that and will either have to step back or fall down. If you lightly grip his chin and complete the arc by moving your arm down, he'll fall over."

"Really?"

He nodded. "So you push like this." He demonstrated on himself. "Now, you try."

We practised the first motion whilst we sat down, then Jay had us stand up, so I could practise pushing him off balance before getting him to start falling over. Everything was practised slowly. Jay said that if we did it fast, it would definitely make him hit the ground hard. The staff watched us curiously, with amusement. Jay grinned at them. I smiled, sitting self-consciously down again.

"Is that Aikido?" I asked, recalling how Jay had once tried, in a fit of great enthusiasm, to get me to join his Aikido class. He'd practised it all through Tech, as far as I could remember.

"Yep."

"But this is easy! Not like that stuff you were doing when I came to class with you that time."

He smiled with a trace of that old enthusiasm. "It's not hard once you get to practising it."

I doubted that. They'd been doing these rolls and falls, rolling over and standing up in one motion, being thrown and still landing on their feet, and moving in these circles that made me dizzy just watching them. Never having been an athletic person myself, I lacked the courage to even try a class. I'd thanked a disappointed Jay and remained a sports-free person. "Do you still practise?"

He nodded. "Never actually stopped. It's great fun."

Thinking back to that class of his, I could see why he'd think so. His face, then, had been one of delight when not one of concentration. I remembered Mike again. "I thought Aikidoists weren't suppose to hurt people."

"Well, *ja*. It's more about subduing your opponent and buying enough time to run away—that's what our teacher, Martin, always said anyway. "I think..," he went on in deep reflection.

"Hmm.?"

"I think..." he didn't finish the sentence, just grinned one of his mischievous grins.

Knowing Jay, I grinned back.

"Are you thinking what I'm thinking?"

"Narf!" I replied, loving *Pinky And The Brain* as much as he did. We both laughed.

"We've had some really good times, haven't we?" Jay sounded strangely uncertain.

"The best!" I smiled back.

"And the worst?"

I shook my head, grinning back. "That would have been when you left and I got stuck working with BandAid Bill!"

He guffawed. BandAid Bill had been so named by Jay for his habit of persistently wearing sandals or going barefoot despite constantly stubbing his toes on low surfaces around the advertising offices.

This left us all with the disgusting, but vaguely entertaining sight of observing his toes turn different colours, and predicting which toe would next sport a Band-Aid. I wouldn't have minded him so much if he hadn't been such a moronic male chauvinistic pig as well. Jay couldn't stand him either, often going great lengths to avoid him.

"I'm so sorry! I didn't mean to," apologised Jay, a few years too late.

I shrugged.

"But we had some great times, heh?"

"*Ja*," I agreed wistfully, half missing that younger, seemingly carefree, time.

Jay leant forward. "Sammi, there's something I've been meaning to talk to you about."

I could see he was serious. This was important to him. "Yes?"

"You know," he began, more hesitant than I'd ever remembered seeing him. "That...You know me better than anyone else. You understand me. I've always appreciated you for...seeing the best in me, too!"

"Jay..."

He held up a hand to indicate he hadn't yet finished. "I've never gotten 'round to saying thank you...for keeping me sane."

"But I didn't do anything!" I protested, in amazement. I had absolutely no idea what he was talking about, only suspecting that it might have something to do with the unhappiness I used to sense in him back at Tech and at the ad agency.

"Oh, you did more than you could've possibly imagined. You—" He stop, staring fixedly behind me, reminding me of a rabbit caught in a headlamp.

A heavy hand fell on my shoulder. I tried to shrug it off, half-turning, with a frown, wanting to show Terry my annoyance. But it was Henry standing there, looking down at me.

* * *

"Hello Samantha. Such a pleasure to see you again."

His greeting sounded warm and sincere, his hand still heavy on my shoulder. His other hand was covered by his jacket. I sat petrified, suspecting the worst.

"That's right, honey." He was watching my stricken stare at his hidden arm. "There's a gun trained on your friend over there. As you know well, I never miss." His tone hadn't changed, casually friendly.

Jay swallowed, but managed to find an even voice. "Grierson's here with backup. If you try anything—"

"Grierson's at the service entrance setting up his little trap. Finding you here is much more convenient for me," smiled Henry.

"If you—," Jay started to say in a low voice.

Henry laughed pleasantly. "If I what, you'll what?"

Jay's eyes moved from Henry's to the gun again. I wished Terry was here. He'd have been able to deal with Henry—gun or no gun.

Henry was smiling smugly at Jay. "You'll both come with me now. No tricks or we don't know who won't get hurt."

Jay exchanged a look with me. I was past being terrified of Henry by now. I'd been in that place too many times these past few days. Jay's gaze was reassuring. He was afraid, but in control. He nodded at me. I knew what he'd have liked to have said: "Everything's going to be okay." I fervently hoped so. We both stood up slowly. Henry was still just behind me.

He took my arm beneath my elbow. "Shall we?"

Jay's expression was strange; a mixture of vulnerability, sorrow —and something else I couldn't quite name. But he wasn't looking at me. He was looking at Henry. I suddenly understood. My breath caught in my throat. He'd made an irrevocable decision. I was instantly more afraid for Jay than for me. *What was he planning?* We turned to leave. Jay's phone rang. We both looked at Henry.

"Get it, please."

Henry stepped closer to me, his back to the entrance and the waitresses at the front, his gun digging into my waist.

Jay dropped his gaze. "Grierson?"

Terry rumbled indistinctly on the phone. Jay looked up at Henry, who stepped even closer in to me. I had the urge to push him away and run, but the gun was a painful reminder of what being shot felt like. My wound, on my other side, was stinging again in sympathy. I didn't want to be hurt any more. I wanted Henry hurt this time —badly.

"We're at the Wimpy having coffee." Jay paused to listen. "Yes, we'll be there." He put his phone away as Henry looked querulously at him. "Grierson wants us at the service entrance in ten minutes."

Henry smiled, "You'll be late, won't you?" He laughed at his *double entendre* and nodded us towards the exit.

Henry indicated Jay should walk on my right. He stuck close to me, his arm brushing mine, leading us at a fast walk away from the service entrance side of the mall.

We were passing a wooden bench, with the walkway not very busy, when it happened. Jay's hand wrapped unexpectedly around my upper wrist, my feet shooting out from under me not a second later. I felt myself starting to fall, but Jay was stepping out and around, dragging my arm with him. I was flying down and around, away from Henry; away from the gun. Vaguely, through my surprise, I thought of merry-go-rounds. Jay let go of my arm, leaving me sitting gently on the floor, looking up at him in a half-daze. Things seemed to be happening in slow-motion.

Jay's movement had ended with him standing next to Henry's gun hand. Both his hands shot out to grab Henry's wrist and gunhand. Jay twisted. Henry's shriek of pain echoed through the mall as he sank to his knees. He tried to stand up again, but a small movement from Jay had him back on his knees, face gnarled in pain. The gun had dropped nerveless from his hand. Jay kicked it under the bench, never loosening his grip on Henry, their eyes locked. Then Jay slammed Henry's arm against the bench edge, snapping the bone with a nasty sound. In almost the same instant, his booted foot smashed into Henry's face, heel first. Henry's features seem to disintegrate into blood. He burbled another scream, collapsing slowly onto the tiled floor. Jay had already pulled out his phone and was calling Terry. With his free hand, he hauled me up to my feet.

"You okay?"

I nodded, stunned. I couldn't believe I was totally unhurt! And what Jay had done...

A security guard was running over, hand going to his baton. We heard Jay say, "Inspector Grierson, we have Henry with us." The guard slowed his pace. Everything was under control.

* * *

Terry had given Henry the professional once over while Jay and I observed the paramedics carrying the accountant off on a stretcher accompanied by two policemen. Then Terry turned his squint-eyed attention to Jay, assessing him. Jay returned his look levelly.

"You took a big risk tackling him, Duart. He could have shot you both if you hadn't been so lucky."

I opened my mouth to say I didn't think luck had anything to do with it, but Jay got in before me.

"A bigger risk than waiting for him to shoot us?"

Terry didn't answer, just stared back at him for a moment before looking down at me sitting on the bench, trying to avoid Henry's blood. He squatted down by me. "How are you doing? Are you hurt?" His concern appeared genuine.

"Fine." I nodded. "Are you going to arrest Henry now, for trying to kill us?"

He nodded. "*Ja*. Kidnapping, intent to kill, and when I get a confession of Lionel's murder, murder in the 1st degree. He won't see the outside world till he's in his eighties, if he lives that long."

"So, it's finally over?" I felt only relief.

"For Henry, yes." His eyes seemed brighter, hypnotically green. "But not for us I hope."

I jerked my head up at him in surprise.

He continued, "I'm sorry about all of this, but..."

"If it hadn't been for Jay." I completed his sentence.

He nodded once, glancing over to Jay who stood to the side, hands in pockets, looking down at us through those long eyelashes of his. "If it hadn't been for Jay...," repeated Terry in a completely different tone.

Jay's look sharpened on him. I felt only puzzled. I sensed the undercurrents but couldn't decipher them, yet.

"Samantha," Terry took both my hands in his, his voice gentle and intimate, "I really want to see you again. I think I've fallen in love with you."

I stared dumbly back at him, then glanced up quickly to search for Jay's eye to see what he was making of all of this, but he'd ambled off to talk to another policeman. Terry was still looking at me with those wonderful eyes, imploring me.

"Please." he added simply.

I thought about what Mary had said as he waited for my response. I thought about what Jay had said, too. Terry's hands felt warm and slightly rough, making my skin tingle. I just didn't know what to think. "Erm...Give me some time."

"Okay." He squeezed my hands and gave them a gentle pat. "I'll call?"

I nodded. He smiled wistfully, ran a light finger along my face, then went off on police business.

I watched his tall, sturdy form retreat, oozing vitality and sex appeal, all the women's eyes following him. Every girl's dream guy. I couldn't imagine why he'd want me...But it seemed he did. Maybe this was the 'something good' that would come into my life from this whole insane business.

~ 12 ~

HOME

"Are you going out with him?" Jay was driving us down to Durban again.

I thought about it; an image of Terry's handsome face in my mind's eye. Jay shot me a quizzical look.

"I dunno." I sighed.

Jay waited expectantly, one of his favourite songs filling the gap. I hummed along, wondering what it might be like to go out with Terry—if there'd be any future in it.

"I don't think he's the guy for you."

I stared at Jay in surprise. "Why? I know you don't like him. And he can be very...abrasive. But..."

"You really like him, don't you?"

"Yes."

"You're falling in love with him." Jay's eyes were fixed on the road again as it became a three-lane, with two trucks in the first and second lanes, slowing us down as we reached the fast lane.

"I don't know about falling in love with him," I hedged. "But I'm certainly attracted to him. And he seems to be attracted to me."

"You're in love with him." Jay's voice was accusing now.

"Well, maybe I am."

He snorted in derision.

"What?"

He glanced at me, his eyes a curious blend of light and shadow. "I'd never thought you'd fall for his type. You've always made fun of them."

"What type? Tall, dark, handsome and successful?"

"You know, Sammi. The Alpha-male ultra-bossy do-things-my-way-or-hit-the-highway kinda guy with a flashy look-at-me car. And he's violent."

The 'And so are you' hung between us unsaid. "*Ja*, well. He looks like he might make a good father and husband."

"He'll suffocate you—your creativity and independence." Jay seemed sure of his prediction.

I rationalised it away. "There has to be some sacrifice for a marriage to work."

"What will he sacrifice for you, do you think? His car, his freedom, his work? Assuming, of course, that he *is* the marrying to stay faithful type."

"Jay!" I was beginning to get irritated and angry, extremely rare feelings towards Jay. "Why are you being so negative? This is the first guy who seems to want to be with me. Give him a chance!"

Jay opened his mouth then shut it with a snap. He changed down for the steep hill, flooring the accelerator, changed down once again to pass a car which had moved into the second lane; then we were back in the middle lane, moving up to 5th gear again. "I just don't want you to get hurt, that's all. I don't trust Grierson not to.

"Oh, Jay." I was touched. I would have hugged my old friend if he hadn't been driving.

We passed Camperdown.

"I'm going to Norway," Jay remarked, as we approached the Assegai off-ramp.

"Really? When?"

"At the end of the month."

"That's great! You going on one of those cruises?" I half-turned to face him.

"No. I'm moving there. I've been offered a job at a research facility."

I took a moment to digest this, somewhat shocked. "But, I thought you were happy at the university. You said, last time, that you're probably going to stay in academia."

"Yeah, well, things change. And this job in Norway is a wonderful opportunity."

"That's good. I'm so happy for you." And sad for myself. I hadn't realised how much I'd miss him. After these past few days, I'd assumed (and promised myself) that I'd visit Jay more often. "What will you be doing?"

"Managing and monitoring the bacteria levels at an experimental energy plant."

"Really?" I was intrigued. "How are they going to produce energy with bacteria?"

"They aren't exactly." Jay was lightening up with a smile. "They're using sewerage—an infinitely growing resource—to generate energy."

"Methane?" I hazarded a guess.

"Not bad for a Chem-almost-flunkie!" praised Jay, pleased. "*Ja*, the bacteria produces the methane. The methane is used to heat boilers. The steam produced is conducted towards huge turbines. So is cool air. The steady wind generated turns the turbines. *Voilà!* Electricity! Clean, renewable, cheap." He grinned widely. "It's going to produce shitloads of money!"

I laughed. I was going to miss him. I told him so.

"There's always email and Skype," he replied.

But it wouldn't be the same and we both knew it.

Jay dropped me off at my parents on the way to see his own. Mum and Dad were glad to see him, as always. He didn't stay long, just for some coffee.

"I've still got lots of stuff to do." He was apologetic.

I walked him to the Mini, the air heavy with things unsaid.

"Jay," I tried, "I don't know what I'd have done—"

"It's nothing. What are friends for anyway?" He was opening the car door.

"You risked your life for me. You got hurt because of me. It's hardly nothing!"

He just shrugged, grinning. "Maybe I just like being a fair lady's knight."

"I guess you do." We hugged awkwardly. "Are you flying through Jo'burg to Norway?"

He shook his head. "I'm flying out of King Shaka. Spending some time with the folks before heading off to the far north. They'll never visit me there. Too cold."

I nodded sadly. "Then I might not see you again for ages."

"You'll always be welcome to visit, provided..."

I looked up at him sharply.

"...provided you aren't followed by gun-wielding accountants!"

I laughed. "God! I hope that never happens again! Keep me posted, okay?"

"Okay."

We hugged again, Jay's breath brushing my hair. He kissed my forehead tenderly, got into his Mini and drove off without looking back.

* * *

I got a couple of stress-free days being spoilt by Mum and Dad.

Terry had called on the first day to check that I was fine and tell me he'd gotten a confession out of Henry for murder and intent to kill. I'd be required to testify at the trial. Henry's confession was a surprise to me. He hadn't seemed the type. I carefully refused to think about the methods Terry might have employed to get his confession. I was just glad the nightmare was over and I could resume my normal life. I contemplated calling Jay, but didn't want to disturb him during the conference. I thought a lot about him those few days, almost as much as I thought about Terry.

Getting back to work was a little strange, with the vague feeling of something missing. I wondered if it might be Jay or Terry—laughing with Jay, and the excitement of being in Terry's presence. I felt like I'd changed so much. Looking in the mirror revealed a slightly haggard-looking face. My body had a few bruises, and the bullet wound was healing beautifully. It had stopped itching continuously in Clarens, so much so I'd almost forgotten it was there. People were kind at work, treating me as if I'd lost a beloved: considerate, but gossipy. Everybody wanted to know the story. Rina and Lindi ushered me off to an early lunch to get all the details.

"So, he just shot you?" Lindi was disbelieving, and Rina wide-eyed.

"Well, technically, he shot Lionel, Terry's brother, and I was standing behind him."

"The bastard!"

"And this Lionel guy died?" Rina was frowning in concern.

I nodded.

"And Terry, the policeman, is his twin brother?"

I nodded again, tasting my favourite panini, incredibly glad I could enjoy it still.

Lindi's eyes were bright with curiosity. "So, this Terry, he saved you, right?"

"Well, actually, it was Jay who—"

"What's he like?"

"Jay's—"

"No, this Terry person." Rina and Lindi were both leaning in eagerly now.

"He's..." I took another bite, chewing thoughtfully.

"Sammi! C'mon! He's hot, isn't he?" declared Lindi.

I couldn't help but smile a little.

"He is!" Lindi hit the table jubilantly. "Come sweetie, tell Aunty Lindi everything! Leave nothing out."

Rina was grinning, equally excited.

I swallowed. "Well, he's tall-ish. Brown hair. Green eyes—real green, not hazel. He's on the broad side. Nice voice: deep, but not Darth Vader deep. He's got a nice smile, but most of the time he looks stern. He's very fit and drives an Audi—"

"Stationwagon, sedan or coupé?" quizzed Lindi.

"A3."

"Ooh!" She was beaming with approval. "Go on."

"Yes! Is he married? Does he have any children? You know so many guys do these days," added Rina.

"No, I don't think he has. He's never been married, never mentioned children."

"How old is he?"

"Late thirties."

I took the opportunity to take another bite of panini as Rina and Lindi thought of more questions. They exchanged a look. The big one was coming.

"Did he say, or indicate in any way, that he might be interested in you?" said Lindi carefully.

I swallowed again, and took a sip of water. "He said he's falling in love with me and wants to see me again. He said he'd call."

"Has he?" Rina asked with bated breath.

I nodded, smiling widely.

"Yeeaahay!" yelled Lindi, scaring the pigeons and bringing out Mielies, the owner.

It took another day to get back to the proper rhythm of my life. Then it felt like I'd never been away; that the whole nightmare had happened to someone else. Jay called once, checking to see if I'd reached Joburg safely and that everything was fine.

"Sammi?"

"Mm...?"

"You be careful, okay. I don't think this thing is over yet."

"But Henry's in jail."

"I know. All the same, just be careful, alright?"

"Alright."

"If you need me for anything..."

"I know." I was smiling. He was such a sweetie.

"Grierson called?"

"*Ja*, he did. He's coming up to Jo'burg on Thursday for the first court appearance. They're transporting Henry up on Wednesday night."

"That's good."

And suddenly, there was nothing else to say.

"Well, bye then. See you when I see you."

"*Ja*. See you when I see you...Jay?"

"Hmm?"

"I'm really going to miss you."

"*Ja* right!" he disagreed, and cut the call with a chuckle.

I was still smiling, a bit sadly, wishing I could see him again.

* * *

Rudely awakened by my ringing phone at about 4am that Thursday morning, I snuggled further down under the covers, reluctant to stick my hand out in the pre-dawn Highveld chill. It stopped eventually. I sighed, settling down to snooze for the next hour or so before the alarm went off. The phone rang again, insistently. Resigned, I stuck out an exploratory hand, gripped the phone and dragged it under the covers. "Hello?" I mumbled half to myself.

"Samantha."

I was instantly alert. "Terry?" My stomach sank with fear. Something was horribly wrong.

His tone was strained with anger. "Samantha, Wilkins was killed on his way up to Jo'burg. It wasn't an accident. I'm coming to fetch you. Pack a bag. I'll be there in forty minutes."

"But..!" I protested.

"Be ready. I'm taking you into protective custody. Don't open the door for anyone else but me."

"But..!" I almost wailed.

"Samantha, there's no time to argue! Just do it!"

I was shocked into silence. No-one had ever spoken to me like that before.

"I love you," he said suddenly, just before he cut the call.

I let the phone slip from my fingers. It wasn't fair! This whole thing should have been over with Henry in jail. Why was it still pulling me in? I should have been completely out of it by now. Protective custody, Terry had said. That meant he believed whomever had killed Henry would try to kill me, too. But why? And more importantly, who?

I jumped up, had the quickest shower I'd ever had, and packed a bag. I used the same one I'd used the previous week, first dumping the contents onto my bed before repacking. Lionel's torch fell out, forgotten in the danger of all that had followed. I stared at it, feeling that same sense of muted horror as I had when it had lain the lodge floor. I would have to give it back to Terry. I stuck it back into my backpack and hastily continued packing.

* * *

Terry pulled up to the driveway gate thirty-five minutes after calling. I was already pressing the button to open the gate before he could press the buzzer, having been on the lookout for him whilst packing, and then standing anxiously at the window. The Audi swished around to my door, the tyres sounding oddly loud in the morning hush.

Terry was out, boot opening, almost before the handbrake had taken, leaving the engine running. "Ready?"

I nodded, handing him my bag, before going back to lock the front door. Terry had turned the car to face down the drive by the time I reached it. I got in as quietly as I could, closing the car door with a click, not wanting to disturb my neighbours.

"You alright?" He released the brake.

I nodded. "And you?"

He nodded back, rolling us towards the gate. I pressed the remote, allowing us out, then turned back to check the gates were shutting properly behind us.

"I'm sorry, Sammi."

"It's not your fault. What happened, anyway? Why do you think I'm in danger?"

He was silent for a few moments, intent, but not on the quiet morning roads. "The convoy carrying Wilkins and another prisoner was attacked last night near Pinetown. Two guards and Wilkins were killed. The other prisoner was not. We're still trying to piece together the details, but it all points to a professional hit. Very professional. I'm afraid you might be next."

"But why me? I don't know anything!"

"If someone's tying up loose ends, you're one of them. They might think you know a lot more than you do."

"And Jay. Have you warned Jay?"

He nodded again. "Yes. He's been warned he might possibly be in some danger. Though you're the one they'll probably be after."

I felt less than reassured at that. "Where are you taking me?"

"You'll see."

And that was all I was able to get out of him just then. I thought of Jay instead, feeling my worry grow. "I'm going to call Jay."

"Okay."

Jay's phone went direct to voicemail.

"When did you call Jay?"

"Right after I called you?"

"Did it go to voicemail?"

"Yes. I assumed he was sleeping."

"Probably." I said it with more hope than certainty. "I'll try him again later."

Terry glanced at me. "Okay. But once you're at the safe-house, no calls."

I opened my mouth to protest.

"I've already called your parents and boss. They've been apprised of the situation."

I tried calling Jay every ten minutes after that for the next hour and a half, hoping he'd answer his phone as we drove through most parts of Joburg. Jay never answered and didn't reply to my texts. My worry grew.

* * *

The safe-house proved to be somewhere on the DusRand just outside Pretoria West. Terry took us up a bumpy gravel road running up between the Magaliesberg and the DusRand. It looked like someone's summerhouse with a thatched main-house and a few outbuildings, including an additional outdoor toilet. One of the outbuildings had an attic space that appeared to house a small communications hub.

"For monitoring the Internationals," explained Terry, as I stared at the aerials with massive lightning rods bristling behind the building.

The main centre was in the main-house. People plugged into their computers were evaluating data and monitoring surveillance cameras and the like. Terry swept me through these stations into the living area. There were four en-suite rooms. I was given one in the middle.

"You can stay here safely until all this is over."

"Grierson!" someone yelled from the operations area.

"I have to go. You'll be fine here?"

I nodded. He touched my hair briefly, then headed back down the hall, the person still calling for him.

I shut the door on the office-type sounds coming from the operations centre and looked around the room. It could have been a B&B—spacious and well appointed. I sighed, deciding to regard it all as an enforced holiday. Collapsing onto the big bed and sinking into the puffy duvet, I wished I'd been able to hear Jay's voice, just to know he was okay. I was surprised at how much I needed to know that he was was.

I dozed off lying there, only to awake a while later to the oddest feeling that I'd just spoken to Jay and that he was fine. It was a strange, yet comforting feeling. I hung on to it.

* * *

There wasn't much for me to do at the safe-house, except sleep, eat, watch TV and read. Terry dropped off some books and magazines for which I was grateful.

"Thanks," I smiled at him, then went over to my bag to pull out Lionel's torch. "This was... I...er... kind of picked it up when I...when I ran away from Lionel that night. I...never got a chance to return it. I thought you might like to have it."

Terry stared at me, then at the torch.

"I'm sorry," was all I could say, wringing my hands a little.

He nodded, finally accepting it, before leaving without a word.

My meals were brought to me in time with the soapies. Much to my horror, I found I was starting to follow the plots. I briefly contemplated writing to *Isidingo* or *Egoli* to suggest my story as a plot-line. Something for the future, I mused.

I had no idea how long I'd have to stay in the safe-house—in limbo. Terry had said it would all be over once they found out who'd killed Henry and why. He hadn't yet mentioned, when he spoke to me (at least once every day), whether there'd been any progress in the investigation. I took it to mean there was none. The nasty thought that this was going to be another one of those many unsolved crimes crept into my mind. I might never get my life back...How long would Lucy hold my job before being forced to appoint someone new? It was hard not to feel depressed.

And at the back of my mind, worry about Jay hovered. Was he truly safe? Or had he been killed; lying dead somewhere? I asked Terry to look into it. He said that he would, but had seemed busy and distracted, obviously not registering it as a priority.

One night, I caught a programme on SA Rock. They played one of Jay's favourite Sugardrive songs, *Interplanetary MVA*. I fell asleep sobbing that night, having never felt so alone and uncertain. It was a strange night. I woke up every few hours feeling exhausted, snatches of vague dreams in my head whirling around before I'd fall asleep again. I'd swear that Jay was in one of them, telling me that all was fine, and that I was not to worry. But it was just a dream... I needed something more concrete. And a sense of purpose.

The next morning, after being handed my requested pen and a notebook, I began writing down all that I knew about the matter; everything I could remember down to the smallest detail; and all that had been said to me—Mary, Lionel, Henry, Terry, Jay and Inspector Govender.

I found that when it came to Jay I was writing stuff at the back of the book. Things he'd said and impressions I'd gotten, that thinking about it now, didn't quite add up, or added up to something different to what I'd thought it to be. I refused to believe Terry's accusation of Jay being involved with Henry and his accomplices could be true. There had to be another reason that made sense— and I was determined to find it.

* * *

Eventually, I concluded the whole matter came down to that twenty million sitting in that bank account. Someone desperately wanted it. People did a lot worst for a fraction of that much money. I decided to share my conclusions with Terry, just in case it was a help. It made me feel like I was doing something constructive.

"Terry, I've been thinking about this whole thing and I think it's got something to do with the money in that bank account." I said the next time I saw him.

"Samantha, honey, it's good of you, but let us professionals worry about the case, okay?" He'd taken my hand in his, rubbing warmth into them in the chilly room. "We've already reached that conclusion but there's no such bank account that we could find."

"Well, it's hardly surprising, 'cos Jay found out it's actually a bank account password."

Terry stared at me, his hands stilled, holding mine. "What?"

"Jay found out. We met some Swiss people on the way to Clarens—"

"And you never thought to tell me this?"

It was my time to stare at him, with the realisation that I was entering a minefield. Terry obviously knew nothing about this. Telling him how much Jay knew, and how, would be a major mistake. Playing it safe would be best. Terry was still looking fixedly at me, a hint of the menacing Grierson countenance creeping through. "I thought you knew. We told Inspector Govender about it. He said he'd look into it."

"He did?"

"I guess so. Didn't he tell you about it?"

"I haven't spoken to Inspector Govender for some time. I've been too busy to return his calls."

"Oh." I couldn't believe Terry would allow such a breakdown in communication. I could see now that not everyone held as high an opinion of Terry's investigative abilities as Detective Ngcobo. Inspector Govender had been right, Terry was too close to the people in this case. First Lionel and now, it seemed, me...

"What else did Jay say?" Terry's look had intensified.

"Erm..." I was trying to think of something helpful yet non-implicating to say. I settled for: "I can't quite remember. He might have said something about a bank name, but I can't remember it. He spoke to some Swiss tourist guy."

Terry squeezed my hand. "Good. Thanks for telling me all this. I did send out an enquiry on Jay. Seems he's holidaying with his parents. They're on a boat somewhere off the Mozambiquan coast."

"Oh, right. Thanks!"

He kissed me and left. Duty calling, as always.

* * *

It was a relief to hear about Jay. I always forgot Jay's parents had a 40-footer which they sometimes took out of the yacht basin for a sail up the coast. It surprised me that Jay went with them as he hated sailing with his parents. He'd always said that being in a confined space with them drove him nuts. Jay loved his family, but...With Jay's habits and laid-back manner, it was easy to forget his family was actually well-to-do. His mother did the Ladies-who-Lunch bit whilst his father ran successful businesses. Jay was the middle child—like me, though, he'd rebelled a lot more than I ever did. His older brother was in Canada and his younger sister in Australia, both married like my own brother and sister. Jay always claimed he was the normal one and his brother and sister the crazy ones; crazy to settle down with their own families and build a life in new country. But it was Jay who didn't think like other people. He said I was similar. That's what made us such good friends—our mutual rejection of the following the herd mentality.

But maybe it was time for me to join the herd now—with Terry. Not that I thought Terry was a sheep; more like a wolf or a leopard. And Jay? Jay was probably one of those wild free horses—those mustangs you always see in National Geographic films. Not so wild perhaps, but needing freedom, open spaces and new horizons more than he needed companionship and stability.

* * *

The days dragged by. Terry was vaguely attentive. I could tell he was growing more worried and frustrated by the lack of any leads. When I asked Terry if I could go home, he hesitated.

"But there's been no indication that I'm in any danger!" He'd told me earlier that there had been no strangers observing my home or workplace.

"Samantha, I still think you're in danger."

"Terry," I tried to keep my voice as reasonable as possible. "It's been over a week. I need to get back to work. It's a really good job, and I don't want to lose it."

He looked at me, trying to assess how serious I actually was, and the level of importance of it to me.

"Alright. But you'll stay at my place. That way I can protect you."

I stared at him a little dumbfounded. It sounded an awful lot like he was sounding me out on moving in with him!

He caught my expression and smiled. "I promise I'll be a good boy. No pressure. I just want to be close by to protect you, alright?"

"Okay."

"Come here." We hugged.

I thought how lucky I was to have such a man in my life. And to still be alive to appreciate it.

* * *

"Terry?"

"Hmm?" His attention was fixed on the R28 as we flew towards Johannesburg, its twin lanes blessedly clear of the perpetual snarl-backs of the R511 and Centurion Road.

My question for Terry was a difficult one to broach. It had been bugging me ever since the Midlands Mall. I'd been trying to judge his true feelings for me. A part of me, hidden beneath the excited, dizzy one that wanted his attention, couldn't help but think he was just playing with me for some reason; or that I was just some diversion for him so he wouldn't have to deal with the pain and anger of losing his brother. I fidgeted with my sweater hem, rolling it and unrolling it. "I was wondering...?"

He glanced at me. "Yes?"

I took a huge breath. His phone rang.

"Hang on a sec," he said, switching to bluetooth. "Yes?"

With a hmming here and there, interspersed with a curt question from him every now and then, the phone call seemed to be go on for a long time. My question would have to wait until we reached his place, then I'd have his full attention. We turned to join the highway to Fourways, slowing to a crawl in the long evening traffic jam.

~ 13 ~

FINE TRAPPINGS

Terry's place was a little daunting at first. One of those ultra-trendy candidates for a feature on *Top Billing*—so very different from my own place which (at its best) is called eclectic Bohemian, but is more often referred to as student décor. It reflected my love for browsing flea markets and charity shops, both of which suited my pocket perfectly. I hadn't known what to expected of Terry's place but it went very well with the Audi.

The marble-topped ultra-modern kitchen, complete with recessed lighting, greeted me like a cold mother. The silk Persian carpet, lounging elegantly by the expensive-looking stone fireplace decorated with ethnic art pieces, seemed to cast me a disdainful glance before ignoring me at a swish party. I felt utterly self-conscious, cowering into myself. This was a mistake. I wanted my own shabby, homely stuff.

Terry laughed. "Don't look like that. Just relax and make yourself at home." He surveyed his place leisurely, as if seeing it for the first time, then turned to me. "I hardly spend much time here. All that travelling. So please, excuse the not-lived-in look!"

That said, he kicked off his boots onto the Persian carpet and padded on socked feet up the wooden spiral staircase with my bags. Sighing, I followed. Four doors upstairs lead off an octagonal landing with a huge French window. Terry emerged from one of the doors on the left and conducted the tour.

"This is the study. You can use the internet in there."

He opened the first door to the right and let me have a peek in. Floor to ceiling dark wooden bookshelves, another red Persian, and a dark wooden desk greeted me. A silver-towered AppleMac winked conspiratorially in the dimness.

"And this is you." He ushered me in.

A huge sleigh-bed, yet another Persian, two Bosch oils and a large Boesman (oil again) dominated the huge room. An enormous window and an en-suite completed it. My bag lay lost on the carpet looking forlornly back at me. Terry had opened the bathroom door to reveal a large spa-tub amidst wood and glass.

"But, Terry, this is your room!" I protested.

He grinned. "I thought you'd like the tub. It's fine. I have a nice shower. See..." and he led me over to the last door to where he'd sleep.

It was also a large room, slightly smaller than the main, complete with another huge bed, a small chest, a smaller window, two smallish Munro's with their distinctive tulips, and an en-suite, with a decent-sized shower sporting one of those massage heads.

"Are you sure. 'Cos this is more than fine for me."

"Don't be stupid. I want you to be comfortable." He pulled me in for a long embrace. "You hungry?"

"Hmm hmm."

"Debonairs?"

I smiled. It had been ages since I'd last had pizza. I nodded eagerly.

* * *

"What will you have, tea or coffee?" asked Terry as we waited for the pizza to be delivered.

He appeared slightly awkward in the role of host, now that we were left to talk. It was obvious he wasn't used to having people over at his place despite all the hospitality trappings.

"Coffee, please." The autumn chill had decided me. I didn't usually have coffee this close to bedtime.

"Right!" stated Terry, looking around his hardly-used immaculate kitchen before going into surprising action. Out came a silver coffee machine that looked like it had cost my whole month's salary. He set the contraption to warm up after adding mineral water to boil. Next, from a drawer of carefully lined jars, he pulled out a vacuum labelled one and opened it. The aroma of rich, decadent coffee filled the air. Measuring carefully, he dropped the beans into the coffee machine. With a flourish he grabbed two mugs to set them under the twin spouts. Only then did Terry look at me to gauge my reaction. I quirked an eyebrow and smiled to show how impressed I was.

"Milk?" he remembered. I shook my head. He smiled his sudden smile. "Sugar?"

"Three please."

"Dark and sweet," he grinned, remarking, "...like me."

I raised my eyebrows. "You like your dark side then?"

"Keeps me interesting," he grinned.

I tilted my head to consider him. Terry was watching the machine again, lost in his own thoughts as the machine hissed at us. After a minute or so, it decanted its rich twin streams of steaming coffee. Terry came out of his reverie, removed the mugs, added three sugars to one mug and four to the other. He set a mug before me then straddled a bar stool across from me.

"So what is it that you wanted to talk to me about, Samantha?"

I took a moment to phrase the question. "Well, Terry. I...," Shifting suddenly, feeling uncomfortable on the tall barstool, I started over. "It's like this. We've only known each other for a week or two...and we didn't even get off to a good start. I just feel..."

"You think we're moving too fast?" His voice was flat, but he wasn't upset.

I nodded. "And...you're already talking about marriage and stuff, but you couldn't possibly know me well enough to decide on such an important thing. And..."

He was just looking at me with affection, letting me waffle on.

"And, I can't help but wonder if your feelings for me aren't...masking other feelings you don't want to face...about Lionel." There. It was said. I waited for him.

He gazed at me for a moment or two, then gave a short laugh. "It's your honesty I love best, Samantha," he said simply. "I don't get to meet to many people like you. So transparent, so good, so without...the need to tramp on someone else to get what you need. And what you need is not what other people need."

I looked at him in surprise. "And what do I need?"

"You need someone to take care of you. To love you for your simplicity."

I blinked. I'd never considered myself as the sort of woman who needed someone to take care of her in the normal course of life. I could earn my own money, meagre though that may be in comparison to many around me, and I could do all the things living in Johannesburg teaches you; like changing light-bulbs and when to call the security company. And he thought I was simple. I'd always considered myself a complex character as only a middle child could be. But maybe his world was a lot more complicated than mine. Was I overthinking everything again—one of my many flaws of which Terry was probably unaware? Or did he even care about my flaws?

He chuckled again, reaching out for my hand. "You know, Samantha, I never thought I'd tell you this—not so soon anyway—but, once I could see the kind of person you are—your honesty, your bravery, I couldn't help but fall for you. I may have appeared...terse, but only because I was suddenly...terrified!" He grinned at what was probably an old joke to him. "...of losing you! That's a new experience for me. And I know I'm ready to settle down. You're the perfect one for me. We're going to be so happy together. I'm going to give you all the things you've ever wanted. You'll see." He squeezed my hand.

I squeezed back, not doubting his feelings for a moment. Terry truly believed he loved me. All I had to do know was to figure out if I felt the same way about him.

* * *

The pizza was demolished soon after its arrival. We sat in companionable silence for a while after in front of the fireplace with its electric fire till my eyes began to droop. We said our good nights then, well aware of how close the other would be. The sleigh-bed was extremely comfortable. I dropped off to sleep easily.

Sometime later, a strange smell woke me, making me cough. *Was it a fire?* Getting up in alarm, I hastily pulled on a sweater over my t-shirt and tracks, making my way to the door, calling for Terry. Opening the door onto the moonlit landing, I glimpsed a dark shadow flitting into Terry's room.

"Terry!" I yelled, panic and terror making my heart thunder.

I rushed towards his bedroom, intent on waking him. Before I could reach his door, I was grabbed from behind by an arm around my waist, a hand with a damp cloth covered my nose and mouth almost at the same instant. I struggled best I could, but the cloying smell was too much. I passed out.

* * *

I awoke to the loud drone of an aeroplane's engine, and the shuddering of its carriage under me. It was a small aircraft, not a commercial flight. I lifted my head groggily, only to have that cloth cover my nose and mouth again.

***

I drifted hazily into consciousness. Muzzily, I looked around. I was in an attic room with dormer windows. Standing up from the camping bed on weak limbs, a few wobbly, tentative steps brought me to the window. The room was stuffy and hot.

Shaking my head against a dull headache, I squinted through the dirty glass. The window overlooked a large manicured garden.

In the far distance, through the branches of a tall palm tree, I could see a ship on the sea. Unmistakably familiar from my earliest childhood, the Maharani Hotel stood proudly marking the beachfront just before the expansive flat roof of the ice rink. To the right, Greyville Racecourse wound itself around an open green. I sighed in recognition. I was back in Durban, somewhere on the Ridge. So close to the safety of my family, yet so incredibly far away.

I leant against the glass, feeling its coolness beginning to clear my head. I stood there for a while, not thinking, just being. A large hadeda squawked, flitting past like some hellish demon. Startled, I took a step back. I'd have to get out of here. Get a message to Terry, somehow... I checked my pockets. Empty, except for a couple of tissues. The room had nothing of use either, just the shaky camp bed. The door was solid wood but old.

I listened carefully, trying to hear if my captors were in the house. Nothing. Taking a deep breath, I kicked at the door. It didn't bulge. *Perhaps, the lock...* I took a step back, then a quick step forward, kicking out at the lock, just as I'd seen in the movies. The lock rattled. The door failed miserably to burst open. I lost it then, yelling, kicking, and screaming at the unyielding door in a fury, oblivious to the pain I was inflicting on myself. Panting, I collapsed against the door, as close to despair as I'd ever been. It was then, in the comparative silence, that I heard the footsteps. Two pairs. One heavy, one the tic-tac of high heels. A man and a woman. I edged away from the door, a new fear taking hold of me.

The lock snicked, and I took another step back, before the door burst violently open. Malcolm, the vet, glared down at me, his blue eyes intensely piercing.

"What's all the noise about, then?"

Behind him stood an unamused Sheila or Sheena or whatever-her-name-was, all trace of the mousiness she'd shown during the retreat gone.

"Well hello, sweetie," she drawled. "Surprised?"

I shut my gaping mouth, still stupefied.

"No more noise," growled Malcolm. "Unless you really want to get hurt."

He advance deliberately. I shook my head, cowering back up against the window.

He nodded in satisfaction. "Good."

But he didn't leave, just stared at me coldly. Sheila was doing the same, only with some amusement now.

I hated them both just then. "Wha..," I cleared my parched throat nervously. "What—?"

"What could we possibly want with harmless little you?" interrupted a smirking Sheila. "Wouldn't you love to know?" She sashayed as if she was walking a catwalk to stand behind Malcolm, putting her caressing arms around him and asked softly, "Shall we tell her?"

He hadn't taken his eyes off me. He took a few moments to reply while Sheila stroked his neck. "Sure. Why not?" His feral grin was sudden. "She's not gonna tell anyone."

Sheila pouted in mock disappointment, then shrugged. "Shall I, or will you?"

"You can do the honours, babe, once I've made the call." Malcolm had taken out his phone—a cheap Motorola, mostly likely a pre-paid. He attached a small, round gadget to it and dialled.

"Grierson," came Terry's voice over the tinny, noisy loudspeakers.

Malcolm nodded at the phone, indicating I should speak. I opened my mouth, then hesitated.

"Hello," went Terry again, his tone testy.

Malcolm swiftly stepped forward and slapped me. I cried out in shock, stumbling back.

"Samantha!" Terry's voice was concerned and strained.

Malcolm nodded to the phone again, raising his palm in warning. Sheila's smile was unpleasant, making my cheeks burn even more.

"Terry," I croaked.

"Where are you? Are you hurt?"

"I'm...*oof!*"

It was Sheila who'd stepped forward and punched me in the stomach. I doubled over, unable to breathe, and let myself slump onto the floor.

Malcolm was talking to Terry now with the gadget turned on, giving the smirking Sheila an approving look. "...have your girl. Give us the code and you can have her back."

"I want to talk to her."

"Sorry mate. Code first."

"You're not getting anything until I know she's alive and well. And likely to remain so."

Sheila had stepped over to me again as Terry spoke. She grabbed my wrist and pulled it out and back then twisted. I tried to stifle the scream, but Malcolm had move the phone closer to my mouth.

Terry's hiss of anger carried clearly. "If you hurt her again..."

"As you can hear, she's alive and well enough to scream," Malcolm stated, then cut the call, smiling.

Sheila squatted down, tilting my chin to look at my face. "My, my! Isn't the Inspector sweet on you? Can't imagine why." She laughed, letting go of me, then sashayed back to Malcolm to paw at him.

They kissed noisily for what seemed to be a long while as I tried to get my breathing back to normal.

A minute or two later, Malcolm called Terry again. "Give us the code or we'll send her to you in pieces."

There was a moment's silence before Terry replied. "I'll exchange her for the code. Unharmed, or else..."

"Or what? You'll hunt me down like you did Henry?" Malcolm laughed, amused. "You won't find us."

After another longish pause, Terry simply asked, "Where and when?"

Malcolm already had his answer ready. "Gateway. The movies at 7:30pm. Tonight." He cut the call again, looking pleased, like it had all gone according to plan.

Getting up was painful. I made it only to sitting position as feigned as much weakness as I could, in the hope it would buy me some chance to escape. My two captors kissed showily again.

Malcolm pulled away first. "I have to get to the docks. Get the papers ready. They won't unload otherwise." Sheila pouted again, but let him loose. He looked over to me, grinning evilly. "Have fun!"

Sheila laughed heartily as he left. I didn't like the sound of it. She turned and assessed me as she shut the door on the retreating Malcolm. Moving leisurely, she walked over to the camp bed and sat down, addressing me casually, "I love hurting people. So, just give me the slightest excuse and I will. Will you?"

I shook my head, backing as far against the wall as possible. She was without doubt one of the most evil persons I'd ever met. It was a wonder I hadn't seen it before. But neither had Mary, Vusi, or any others on the retreat. Just what, exactly, was going on? She smiled at me again. I'd never been so afraid of another person, not even Henry. With Henry, there'd always been a chance I could get away. And there had been Terry and Jay, too. Here, I was totally alone with no possibility of help arriving before it was all too late...

~ 14 ~

THE RIDGE

"I've just read your mind, sweetie. You know you're gonna die, don't you? But, you don't know exactly when." She flexed her long-nailed fingers.

I stared at the French-manicured talons imagining the damage they'd inflict.

She smiled in triumph, revelling her power. "I'm guessing all the little possibilities are running through your mind now. How did we find you? And what *possible* reason could there be for all this...drama."

I said nothing.

"Well, don't you?"

I nodded quickly. Anything to placate her and buy me some time.

She continued, admiring her manicure. "It's simple, really. All the answers have been right under your nose—and the Inspector's. Go on. Give it a try. Tell me what you think." She shot me an expectant look.

I cleared my constricted throat. "It's...it's about the money in that bank account. You've been working with Henry. He might have double-crossed you...and Malcolm. Now you want your money."

Her look was of grudging approval. "Not bad. Henry didn't actually double-cross us. He just failed to stay focussed. Hunting you down and getting himself caught was not part of the plan. It was

133

incredibly stupid of him. We couldn't risk the chance of exposure of the whole business during the trial." She paused. "And you and your little friends have been wondering: what business? Care to guess again?"

I thought quickly. "Laundered money?"

She laughed. "That's a bit too obvious, darling. Try again."

"Tax evasion?"

Her belly laugh seemed to fill the room. She was clearly enjoying herself immensely. Good. If I kept her happy, she was less likely to kill me soon.

"I can see you've got a one-track mind. Henry's job as an accountant hasn't much to do with it." She leant closer to me conspiratorially. "Toxic Waste Management." She smiled as she imparted the big news.

My blank look said it all.

She couldn't help but explain. "We're a Toxic Waste Management team, or were until Henry screwed things up. You see...," She went into businesswoman mode, crossing her legs. "Any company, or government, can appoint us to help dispose of their toxic waste. It's so difficult these days to find a hassle-free, clean, cheap solution, and that's what we offer. We take the waste off them, ship it cheaply and dispose of it for them—quietly, with no fuss. It's so easy. We're making a killing!" She smile a professional smile, presentation over.

The ship Malcolm had mentioned; it was carrying toxic waste! "What do you do with the waste? How do you dispose of it?"

She smiled in approval again, pleased I was asking intelligent questions that would showcase her superiority. "Easy. We ship it inland, buy a piece of land, and bury it deep. Safe and easy."

And illegal, irresponsible and dangerous! I couldn't believe anyone could be so stupid. "But the water table—"

"...is not my problem," she finished callously.

I was silent for a few seconds, unable to comprehend such a mindset. I hoped she died of radiation poisoning or tainted water, preferably whilst washing that long chestnut hair of hers! I had to keep her talking. "Did Lionel Grierson find out about your plans? Is that why you had him killed?"

"Ah, yes. The interfering little Grierson twins. As if one of them wasn't enough! Yes. He sold us the land, then went back on the deal once he got wind of our plans for it; how, I don't know. He would have been fine—maybe—if he hadn't tried to stop us."

She'd been rocking on the camp bed, making it squeak. I stretched out my legs cautiously, needing to ease the cramp in them, and to get closer to the bed. I remembered she hadn't locked the door. She didn't seem to pay much attention to my movement, enjoying herself too much with being able to finally tell someone who didn't matter just how clever and rich she was.

"Twenty million doesn't go too far these days," she mused, contemplating a fingernail. "So, it's almost a blessing Henry got himself killed..."

I kicked out at the camp-bed joint with my heel. It rocked for a long second, then tipped over. Before I could think about what I was doing, I was up and through the door. Slamming it shut behind me, I fled down the steep flight of stairs, Sheila's banshee yells following me.

I reached a hall first, leading off into a kitchen, and dithered for a moment whether to find a weapon against Sheila, who I could hear running down the steps now. Fight or flight?

I dived into the lounge with its floor to ceiling glass doors. They were locked.

Glancing back, I found Sheila staring at me, murder in her eyes. I raced towards another window, keeping the sofa between us. She stalked in. My hand landed on a heavy stone statue. Hefting it awkwardly, I heaved it at those doors. It bounced harmlessly off. I hadn't been able to throw it hard enough!

Sheila grinned, all teeth. Then, with a surprising screech, launched a flying kick at me. I ducked down instinctively, sliding along the highly polished floor to pull myself up by the curtains.

Sheila hit the glass door and bounced off it, too, falling clumsily behind the sofa. Feeling the curtains beginning to give from my weight, I yanked them down onto her before running out and into the kitchen. I tried the door. Locked too, but the keys were on the counter.

Desperately, garbling a prayer under my breath, I tried two of them before finding the right one. Now just the Trellidor, a slam-shut with its distinctive key, to go... Sheila had extricated herself from the curtains and was rushing down the hall, just seconds away from me. I squeezed through the Trellidor, twisting to slam it shut behind me. Sheila's scream of rage got the dogs barking next door. We stared at each other for a moment, with equal hate.

I backed off first, dropping the keys into the drain before running for my life. I had to go around the house, the high boundary walls providing no other means of escape. Through the living room doors and windows, I spotted Sheila again. She had a cleaver in her hand and was fitting some keys into the French door. I bolted through the garden towards what I hoped would be a driveway. Thankfully, it wound downhill, enclosed by a small verge and high, white walls. I pounded down the winding drive, adrenalin pumping my legs and heart faster.

* * *

The gate at the bottom was closed. A set of pretty, wrought-iron bars between me and life. I launched myself, unthinking, from a few steps away, clawing and scrambling up it, not even consciously registering the electrified strands strung at the top. I don't know how I did it, but I was over and falling on the outside, to land winded but able to run again. Then, I was almost on the main road, frantically running for help—any help. It found me.

I saw the car coming, but couldn't stop in time. My momentum, and the incline, were too great. I shut my eyes against the inevitable. There was a long, interminable shriek of tyres and smell of burnt rubber. Cold metal bumped against my knees almost gently. I collapsed against the blue bonnet wondering why my legs weren't crushed. Looking up in a daze, I found Jay staring, equally shocked, back at me. Sheila's screech could be heard approaching fast down the drive. Jay and I turned as one to catch a glimpse of her appearing. Spurred into action, I was at the passenger side of the Mini in an instant, which Jay had already thrown open. We were shooting down the road before I could reach for my seatbelt.

"What the hell? You okay?"

It was so good to hear Jay's voice. I could only nod and pant. We swung off to the left, following the curve onto Ridge Road.

"Who was that harridan?"

"Sheila. Or Sheena. Not sure which."

He glanced at me. My breathing rate had halved, but was still nowhere near comfortable.

"Where to?"

"The harbour."

"What!"

"A ship carrying toxic waste is about to be unloaded unless...unless we stop it....It's....what this has all been about."

Jay had that stubborn set expression, his voice almost angry. "I'm not taking you anywhere near the docks. Let Grierson handle this."

"He doesn't know yet."

Jay tossed his phone to me. "Tell him."

I called Terry. It rang and rang. Maybe he wasn't accepting calls from Jay. Or maybe he was still on a flight. Glancing at Jay, I said, "I'll call Inspector Govender."

Jay nodded once.

Inspector Govender listened attentively to my breathless story then asked two questions. "What's the address of that house on the Ridge?"

"I don't know." I looked at Jay, askance.

"Vause Road. Upper 200s. A wrought iron gate about 250m from Springfield."

I relayed it to the Inspector.

"What's the name of the ship?"

"I'm sorry. I don't know that either. But I can identify the man who's bringing the stuff in. He was introduced to me as Malcolm at Mary's weekend in Magaliesberg. He's probably declaring everything as veterinary supplies."

The Inspector was silent for a few breaths as Jay turned down onto the Greyville Racecourse Road. "You can definitely make a positive ID?"

The Inspector's voice carried clearly as we stopped at the intersection on what used to be Cowey Road. I was too tired to read the new name. "Absolutely."

Jay shot me a dark look. He really wanted me safely out of the way somewhere, but I desperately needed to have this whole thing over with. Then only would I feel safe and know I'd done my best to stop a hugely evil thing—no matter how it ended.

"Okay," said the Inspector with a sigh. "I'll call you back in five minutes."

"Thanks." I put the phone down on my lap. "Fives minutes," I informed Jay.

He nodded again.

"Where are we going?"

"Some place that will make our troubles just float away."

"That's nice," I remarked absently, anticipating the Inspector's call. Then we hit the stadium traffic.

I'd finally gotten my breath back as we crawled along with the traffic. It appeared the Bulls were in town. Almost every second or third car had a striped blue or black jersey in it. Jay hadn't said anything else. "I thought you were still somewhere off the coast of Mozambique."

Jay half-tilted his head towards me. "Came back early. Emergency board meeting for Dad, emergency salon appointment for Mum. It's dreadful what saline water and air does to hair colour." From his dry tone, it wasn't hard to guess Jay was once again upset with his parents.

"What were you doing on The Ridge anyway?"

"Driving."

"Jay!"

He gave a secret smile. "Looking for an old friend."

"Oh." With an inexplicable stab in my chest, I wondered if the friend was a she. "Lucky for me you were there."

His smile turned a little sad. "Yes. Lucky for you."

"Look, if you still want to catch your friend, you can just drop me off at the Portnet Building. I'll be fine surrounded by police and security types, most likely...And Terry will probably pitch up soon."

He gave me a very old fashioned look. "You were surrounded by police and security types at the mall. I'm seeing this through with you."

"But, I don't want you hurt. I was sick with worry when we couldn't get a hold of you after Henry was killed. I don't want to go through that again!"

He was silent for a moment. "I got a message I might be in danger, then another that all was fine."

"Terry told you that you weren't in any danger?"

"No, it was my friend, Tom. He's found out some more stuff. I passed it on to Inspector Govender, who also thinks I'm in no danger. Only Henry knew of me. Not the others."

I thought it over a minute. "Your friend found out about this whole business?"

"A lot of it, not all. He couldn't trace these Sheila and Malcolm persons. He did find out about the ship and is trying to trace its name. These ships change names at sea, so it's difficult to track their courses and ports of call."

"You know, if you and Terry shared information this whole business might have been over a whole lot sooner."

"It might not have gotten us Sheila and Malcolm. Besides, I told Inspector Govender. It was up to him to pass it on to Terry. I'm not the police, Sammi."

"Terry doesn't appear to speak to Inspector Govender."

Jay shrugged his shoulders. "Tough."

I sighed and thought my own thoughts.

We were still stuck on Stanger Street on the way to the yacht basin when Inspector Govender called back about fifteen minutes later.

"Meet Inspector Dube at the Portnet building. He has some men on the way and is notifying the port authorities. Go find this guy. And good luck."

Jay glowered at me as I relayed the instructions, but obediently began making his way to the left to change our route.

"You know it's funny, Jay, how you always seem to be there when I'm in danger." I watched his face carefully, wanting to solve this mystery once and for all.

"Yes, isn't it?"

"It's uncanny...Like you just know!"

"Hmm..." He wasn't paying me any attention, focussing on the traffic as it thinned. We picked up speed. "What was that Inspector's name again?"

"Dube."

"Dube," he repeated, still sounding half attentive.

* * *

We reached the Portnet building about twenty minutes later. Inspector Dube came forward to introduce himself as we pulled up. He was a short, slightly portly man with an open, friendly face. He took us up to introduce a Mr Moodley, Harbour Master; and a Mr Francis, Security Manager of the port—a military type. I, in turn, introduced Jay. They unspokenly accepted he was accompanying me. Mr Moodley led us all to the Control Room where we were issued with flak-jackets and binoculars, then informed us of the three possible ships now under suspicion.

"We're just waiting to confirm the cargo manifests. It may take a couple of minutes," Mr Moodley kindly informed us.

I loitered around for a few minutes before walking over to Jay, who stood watching the scene outside through the wraparound windows.

An operator brought up the manifests on screen, then began reading out loud. "The *Morning Star*, registered in Paraguay: cattle vaccinations from the Netherlands. *Alderbaran*, registered in Egypt: dog food and pet accessories from Britain. And *Atlantic Freedom*, registered in the Caymans: veterinary supplies from the UK."

"That might be the one," guessed Mr Moodley. "Let's start there. Where is she docked."

"Maydon north, sir."

"Let's go."

"Sir, you'll follow behind us," Dube instructed Jay as we filed down to the cars. "Stay behind at all times. Should the unexpected happen, get out of there fast!"

Jay nodded.

"Keep in contact with this radio. Press this button to speak."

"Right."

Jay passed the two-way radio to me. It was heavier than it looked. We got into the Mini and took our place in the neatly filing vehicles. There were no sirens. It wouldn't do to scare Malcolm off.

The *Atlantic Freedom* looked deceptively small once we got alongside her. Jay stopped the furthest back, positioning the Mini nimbly so we could race off, if need be.

"Just shout when you see him," crackled Inspector Dube over the radio.

Pressing the button, I said, "Okay," then spied through the binoculars.

Moodley and Francis's party boarded the ship first. Dube and his team were close behind at the end of the gangway. Jay and I sat watching tensely. It took about ten minutes to get the crew and others assembled on deck.

"Whenever you're ready, ma'am," came Dube over the radio again.

I carefully scanned the men through the binoculars. None of them looked familiar. Most seemed to be Filipino or Malaysian. "I don't see him."

"That's fine. We'll move onto the next one."

Dube gave a signal and his men began to disembark. The Portnet guys spoke briefly to the captain and crew, thanking them, it seemed. Then we were off again.

"The *Morning Star* is further along here. We'll go there first," Moodley's voice informed us.

Once again we took our place at the tail of the convoy.

"Think you'll spot him?" Jay shot a quick glance at me.

"God, I hope so!"

Jay sighed.

We drove under gantry crane legs and along streets created by cargo containers. It didn't take long to reach *The Morning Star*. Looking white and new, she seemed much better maintained than *Atlantic Freedom*.

"Keep your eyes peeled," intoned Jay melodramatically.

A familiar-looking *bakkie* drew my eye, almost hidden between two towers of giant wooden crates. It was a Nissan. "I think he's here. I'm sure I've seen that *bakkie* before."

Jay looked sharply at me.

"The plates," I said, looking through the binoculars, "are Northwest Province."

Jay said nothing, just tensed.

I spoke into the radio. "I think he's here. There's a *bakkie* by those crates that might be his."

We followed the same procedure. Jay positioned the Mini so we could make a fast retreat. The Portnet guys and the police boarded the ship. But this time, they immediately requested a search. The crew was assembled on deck again—fewer than the *Atlantic Star*, many of them looking ill. Mr Moodley spoke over the radio to the Portnet building, his worried voice calling for the Paramedics and a quarantine.

Inspector Dube came on immediately after. "Can you see him, ma'am?"

"No, not yet." I'd been watching the ship intently through the binoculars.

Jay scanned the area around us, shifting with discomfort. The *bakkie* was empty, the police had already checked it. *Where was Malcolm?*

A nasty feeling grew. "Jay," I said, still looking through the binoculars, "I'm going to—"

"Don't," he said quietly.

It took a moment for me to realise he wasn't addressing me, his gaze fixed past me, through the window. I swung my head, to stare at Malcolm. He held an evil-looking gun in his hand pointed unwaveringly at my head through the open window.

"Don't move!" he growled.

I moved my finger anyway, pressing the transmit button on the radio hidden by the shadow of the seat against the car door.

"Put your hands on the steering wheel, slowly," he instructed Jay.

Moving warily, never taking his eyes off Malcolm, Jay placed his hands lightly on the steering wheel.

"Good. Now you," Malcolm, looking at me, gestured with the gun. "Get out."

I met Jay's eyes—*Do as he says.*

I let the still broadcasting radio fall down. Malcolm was no fool.

"Turn it off."

I bent to find it, located the switch and did as I was told. Jay still keeping his eyes on Malcolm, didn't move a muscle. He couldn't, not without getting me killed.

"Get out. Slowly," repeated Malcolm.

I opened the car door with half a mind of swinging it hard at him, but he'd taken a couple of steps back with the gun still trained on me. Jay, under such duress, was still unable to help. I took a deep breath. Both my life and Jay's depended on my next actions.

I got slowly out of the car, waiting for an opportunity to act. There didn't seem to be any. Besides, I had no idea of what exactly I should do. I stepped around the open door, bringing myself closer to Malcolm and his gun. *'Jay!'*, I called silently in my mind, *'What do I do?'* I remembered then, the chin-push thing Jay had shown me at the Wimpy. If I got the slightest chance...

'Not yet.' I heard Jay in my mind as clearly as if he'd spoken. His eyes were on me and Malcolm, slightly unfocussed, his body curiously relaxed. *'Wait.'*

Malcolm grabbed my arm roughly, pulling me forward. I staggered towards him, almost falling. *'Good!'* came Jay as Malcolm took a step back to avoid me falling on him. *'Be a dead-weight,'* advised Jay. My next unstable step brought me almost upon Malcolm, who was still just a half step in front of me. *'Now!'* My right hand shot up, cupping Malcolm's chin and pushing. *'Make a circle. Don't grab, push! Complete till he's on the ground.'* The instructions all came as quick as thought. I was following them just as fast. And Malcolm was falling. As I continued the downward chin-push, it seemed natural to push his gun-hand away instead of grabbing for it. In my adrenalised state, Malcolm was taking forever to fall. On its own volition, my left leg went behind his, tripping him. He hit the tar with a whoomph!

Jay was somersaulting out of the Mini, having launched himself over the passenger seat. He landed on his feet, standing on the wrist of Malcolm's gun-holding hand. Malcolm yelled starting to thrash about. Jay knelt down to strike him with the heel of his hand on the chest. Malcolm went still, wheezing for air. I was gasping for breath too, stunned. It had all taken less than ten seconds. Jay and I had won!

"Get the radio." Jay had stood up.

I nodded, stepping around him, leaving him to keep an eye on Malcolm. Getting into the Mini, I groped for the radio in the dimness of the foot-well. A gasp of pain from Jay had me look behind. Malcolm had kicked his knee. Jay's leg was buckling down whilst

Malcolm had rolled up and hit out hard at Jay, who deflected the strike but continued falling. Alarmed, I kicked the car door out, intending on hitting Malcolm. But he spun away, out of range, leaving Jay to face the door. '*Door!*' I opened my mouth to shout, but Jay was already throwing himself back to lay flattened against the tar. The car door swung harmlessly over his long legs. Malcolm ran off, dodging behind some crates. Jay was looking a little startled, hurt and not a little annoyed.

"Sorry! I meant to hit him."

Jay picked himself up and dusted himself off. "So that was Malcolm."

"Jay! I could hear you—in my mind! How?"

He dropped his eyes, a curious expression in them; a mixture of dread, shame, obstinacy, and (even more oddly) triumph. "Not now. Later," was all he'd say.

I wanted to protest, needing an answer, but Inspector Dube and his team were running up.

"Which way?"

Jay pointed. "He doesn't have his gun any more, but he might still have a weapon."

"Wait for us at the Portnet building!" called the Inspector over his shoulder as he and his team gave chase, drawing out guns as they ran.

Jay watched the police disappear in Malcolm's direction. "I hope they catch him."

"I hope so, too!" I agreed fervently, watching Jay.

"Come on." He limped, wincing a little, over to the driver's side.

I was flooded with guilt. "You okay?"

He nodded.

"It looks painful."

"It is, but it will do fine. Don't want it to get stiff."

Men!

~ 15 ~

MAYDON WHARF

Three hours later we were still waiting for news of Malcolm.

The chase had proved fruitless. With the docks being so extensive, there were too many hiding places and too few men. It looked like Malcolm had gotten clean away. But there had been other progress. A thorough search of *The Morning Star* had confirmed the presence of toxic chemical waste in three different containers stored in different parts of the hold. Samples had already been sent to the CSIR to identify the toxins. The ship was now under quarantine along with her crew, and the captain had been placed under arrest.

The illness of the crew, despite the containers being firmly sealed, had given credence to the fact that at least some of the waste was dangerously radioactive. Fortunately, *The Morning Star* had not been in port long and none of the cargo had been unloaded, so everyone was fairly confident the three containers were the only toxic ones the ship had carried.

Jay appeared stony-face at all this news while the Portnet guys kept us up to date with each new cup of coffee and some biscuits. The fact that Malcolm was out there was getting to me, too. Outside, twilight was arriving, which would give way to sudden night as was common in Durban.

I'd tried earlier to talk to Jay about how I'd 'heard' him instruct me on what to do to Malcolm. But he'd stone-walled me again. All he'd said was, "Later. This isn't the time or the place." So, we sat in the boardroom waiting, the silence charged once again with things unsaid. Telepathy was the word running through my mind, but that only happened between twins, right?

I tried to stifle a huge yawn. The long couch looked more and inviting. I stretched out on it, covering myself with Jay's jacket, wishing for a hot shower or heavenly bath. An image of Terry's bathtub flitted into mind. Was that less than 24 hours ago? It felt like a whole other lifetime... I tried to relax; let my mind wander as I do when healing.

On the matching couch, at right angles to mine, Jay appeared totally engrossed in a maritime magazine. I knew somehow, back there with Malcolm, Jay had heard my thoughts and responded to them instantaneously in a way I could comprehend without obvious communication. I had not imagined it. It *had* to be telepathy. I resolved to look more into it when I had the chance. Meantime, I could experiment—give it another try...Like right now.

Jay flipped a page over. I half-closed my eyes, letting my attention wander to him. *'Jay?'* I directed my thoughts as I would my voice. His gazed flicked up sharply to me, then went just as rapidly back to the magazine. *'Well, I'll be...'* I thought lazily. *'You might have told me before.'* Still no apparent response from him. I felt his attention shift to focus on me. He *was* listening to me, telepathically, I knew. *'It certainly explains a lot.'* I continued mutely. He flipped another page over, still feigning obliviousness. *'Could you always do this?'* Still no answer from him, but a small, secret smile crept across his face; his amusement seeming to fill the whole room. *'You bastard.'* His smile grew bigger. I wondered whether I should be angry or amused. Then Terry rushed in, shutting Jay down like a trapdoor with a broken spring. I sat up.

Terry assumed charge immediately. "Samantha? You okay? What the hell happened?" The last, sharply accusing to Jay.

"I'm okay. We found the ship. But Malcolm got away."

"Thanks to him." He jerked his head at Jay. "I heard. What's he doing here?"

Jay decided wisely to ignore Terry and returned to his magazine.

"Jay's been helping me."

"Again? How? How did he find you when you were kidnapped?"

I wondered for a moment how to field that one before replying, "I escaped from the house, running down to the main road, and Jay was driving by."

"Funny," Terry's voice was hard, "how he's always in the vicinity, just like that, eh?"

My eyes met Jay's briefly. "*Ja*. It's funny, but that's coincidences for you. Lucky me."

"Yes. Lucky for you, except for our prime suspect having gotten away again! And here's Jay, as usual, right in the middle of it!"

Jay looked up at Terry. Terry glared down at him.

Here we go again, I thought. "Terry, I told you before. I was the one who brought Jay into this. It's just...totally coincidental that we both happened to be at the same place at the same time. Be reasonable." Terry glanced at me looking imploringly at him.

"Then perhaps he'll be more than happy to explain the forty million in his bank account, fifteen mill of which was deposited not three days ago."

I laughed. "You're kidding, right?"

But neither Jay nor Terry were laughing along. Both looked dead serious. Terry was oozing aggression whilst Jay gave him a level look. Long, tense seconds ticked by.

"I'm calling my lawyer." Jay broke the stalemate, taking out his phone.

Terry knocked it aside. "I asked you a question, Duart."

Jay froze, then stood up with deliberation.

"Guys!"

They ignored me, locked in their battle of wills.

"Are you arresting me?" Steel had crept into Jay's voice despite him being trapped with the sofa behind him.

"I'm gonna find out what I need to know right now, Duart." Terry was back to being the menacing presence I'd first met. "Where'd you get all that money?"

"I don't have to tell you anything," Jay's voice hadn't changed. He was just as formidable, in his own way, as Terry. And Terry apparently hadn't noticed or had chosen to ignore this.

"Jay, please. Just tell him."

He glanced at me, noting the fear in my eyes. Relenting, he spoke to me, not to Terry standing nose to nose with him.

"I sold some property in Schoemansville. I won't be needing it any more."

I stared at him in disbelief. It was just on the opposite, expensive side of the dam to where my sister lived. "You had property in Schoemansville?"

He nodded. "Bought it when I sold the company. It's right on the water. I was lucky..." he smiled almost in apology.

"And you expect us to believe that?" scoffed Terry, with crossed arms, chest puffed out.

Jay gave him a cool look. "Why don't you check it out, Inspector. I'm surprised you manage to solve any cases, with you jumping to all the wrong conclusions instead of investigating. But maybe that takes too long for you, and bullying is easier?"

"Terry!" I yelled, half-stepping forward as he swung at Jay with that powerful fist of his.

Jay merely swivelled around out of the way of that fist to pushed almost gently against Terry's shoulder. Terry, caught off balance, fell harmlessly face first onto the couch, an expression of disbelief spreading across his face.

"Try that again and I'll have you for brutality and harassment, as well as slander, Grierson."

Flashing me a look of apology, Jay walked out.

I stared at Terry lying half on the couch, still trying to comprehend what had happened, and shook my head in exasperation. What was wrong with the man? I followed in Jay's wake. He was talking to Moodley, Francis and Dube. I went to stand by a huge window, listening to the men talk. The harbour lights sparkled in the dark water, almost as if in apology for the muted stars in the light-polluted sky.

Terry came soon after and stood beside me, listening and watching the four men as well. They spoke with animated interest, before purposefully dispersing. Jay turned around and took a step towards us. Terry chose to speak then, lowering his voice intimately.

"Samantha, I'm sorry if all of this has upset you. I wish it could be otherwise. But I love you. I still want to marry you...No, don't say anything yet."

He'd stopped me with a gentle finger over my lips as I started to speak.

"Just think about it." He kissed me thoroughly on the lips.

Behind his shoulder, I could see Jay awkwardly hanging back. And suddenly, Terry was off, without even looking at Jay—like he didn't exist. Jay came over to me then.

"We think Malcolm may still be on the ship. Coming?"

"What? You're actually offering to take me into danger?"

He laughed, shaking his head. "There'll be no danger to you. I'll keep you safe. I promise." He'd said the same thing before...And so had Terry at the mall. But Jay wasn't Terry.

"Okay."

"Come on, then." He jerked his head, smiling, towards Moodley's office where the others were congregating.

We were delayed a few minutes as the news from the CSIR came through. The results were immediately apparent on Moodley's face when he put the phone down and demanded, "I want that ship out of my harbour ASAP! Those containers are highly radioactive. The next tide is at 10:13pm. *The Morning Star* must sail with it!" The operators sprang into action. Nobody wanted radioactive material anywhere near them, not with the World Tourism Conference down the road in three days time.

"Still want to come aboard a radioactive ship?" Jay asked softly beside me.

"If you are, so am I."

He let me lead the way to the car.

"Besides, I've never been on a ship before," I threw over my shoulder.

"Well, it's not exactly gonna be to Starlight standards..."

I grinned.

* * *

The crew and search team arrived almost at the same time as us, looking efficient and able in yellow bio-hazard suiting. Jay and I were issued with the same, giving me the feeling I'd stepped into some episode of *The X-Files*.

"Stay with me," Jay had instructed, before slipping on his head-gear and making Darth Vader breathing sounds.

I giggled. He took it off again, grinning. We went to the bridge first to find Moodley, who was waiting for Jay's ideas. At our arrival, with me awkwardly following Jay through the door, he indicated the schematics of the ship.

"We searched everywhere before. What do you think?"

Jay took a minute to study the schematics. "I think he'd have boarded again after the search. Maybe swam to the ship and entered via the anchor drop. If I were him, I'd hide in the engine room...or the access to the hold. Not many people would be wandering around in there while in quarantine. He doesn't know the ship will sail on the next tide. How long do we have?"

Moodley glanced at his watch. "An hour and thirty-eight minutes."

Teams were dispersed immediately, with repeated warnings on how dangerous Malcolm was.

I stuck close by Jay at the tail end of the team going to the engine room. We filed down narrow, echoing passages made more claustrophobic by the bulkiness of our protective suiting. The surreality of it all hit me. I couldn't help but giggle again. Jay glanced back, and catching my thoughts, flashed me a grin.

We descended two more flights of metal stairs, then along another narrow corridor before we reached the engine room. It took us about fifteen minutes to search the narrow, darkly mysterious grids of the room. With no sign of Malcolm, the hold team was notified. We were asked to join them in the search of the much larger hold. The engine crew who'd elected to sail with the ship, entered as we left, having patiently waited for our search to end.

On the way to the hold entrance, one flight down, the tell-tale shudder of the ship's engines starting told us the engines were in excellent repair. The other search team was making another pass through the hold, just to make sure. Forty minutes later, there was no place else to look.

"Oh well, it was worth a try," said Dube, ending the search.

I turned to follow the policemen, but Jay was dallying a little, looking up through the dimness to the tops of the containers. I couldn't see what had caught his attention. Then he shrugged, and walked over to me quickly.

"Come on," I urged, almost pushing him before me.

We were the last up the stairs to the hold door.

"Remember to close it!" called one of the Portnet guys.

Jay nodded. I'd only just stepped onto the platform in front of the door, when I felt a heavy tug from behind.

'Jay!' I screamed silently, grabbing onto a rail, beginning to topple backwards.

'Dead-weight,' he reminded me, whipping around, his heel snapping out high.

It caught my captor, moving up the stairs, solidly in the face. With a grunt from behind me, I was released. Jay grabbed my hand, hauling me up and to him, stepping back so I was safely off the stairs. Sheena or Sheila or whatever-her-name-was staggered up the last stair. Malcolm dropped down from his hiding place to stand beside her. Jay pulled me protectively behind him as we both backed off towards the exit.

"You alright, hon?" asked Malcolm, eyes glittering as he pulled out a wicked-looking knife.

"He's mine!" snarled Sheila, starting forward, her nose bleeding.

"Run!" Jay yelled out loud.

We pelted down the short corridor. Pausing only to shut the fire-door behind us, we ran down the longer corridor to the stairs leading to the upper decks. Jay pulled me up by a fire-hose, his intentions instantly clear to me. I began turning the wheel to open the valve as Jay pulled out a length of hose and aimed it at the fire-door.

Seconds later, the door burst open with Sheila in the lead, Malcolm right behind her. Desperately, I hauled harder on the valve wheel, willing it to open, now! The resistance lessened all of a sudden, water inflating the hose and shooting out. Jay staggered back almost falling on me. I braced myself against his back to keep us both upright and help him regain his balance. The initial force of the water had hit Sheila in the neck and face, forcing her to stagger backwards into Malcolm. To my alarm, neither lost their footing.

They advanced again, malicious grins on their faces. Jay corrected his balance and adjusted his aim. I leant further into him to give him more stability, simultaneously swinging the valve ring which was now moving much more freely. Jay opened the hose nose fully, letting them have it. Sheila lost her footing first with a cut-off scream, falling onto Malcolm. Jay played the hose on them, not letting them catch their breaths.

We advanced slowly, me supporting Jay, forcing those two back through the door of the hold.

"Shut the door!" called Jay, holding them at bay with the heavy jet of water, feet braced far apart.

Swiftly, jumping over the stream, I slammed the door shut, making sure it was securely locked before collapsing against the wall, breathing heavily.

Jay struggled a for moment to shut off the hose nose, then dropped it on the floor. "Come here."

I hurried to him as he stepped forward. We hugged clumsily in our bio-hazard suiting.

"I think it's finally over," whispered Jay.

"Yes," I mumbled back.

An announcement came over the tannoy. "All crew to report to stations. All visitors to disembark. Ship sails in seven minutes."

I stared at Jay in shock. "What time is it?"

Jay glanced at his watch. The soft shuddering of the ship rose to a juddering for a few seconds as the engines were revved.

"10:17."

"But...!"

He was already pulling me into a run for the stairs.

"They have to catch the tide, get the ship out into the channel. Move!"

~ 16 ~

ON BOARD

I was already running as fast as I could, the dreadful thought of being stranded on board spurring me on. "But, Jay!" I gasped, somewhere just below decks as I halted to catch my breath after a mad dash up three flights of iron stairs. "What about—?"

"We'll tell them when we get off."

Pelting up the last flight of stairs up onto the deck, then racing along it brought us to the starboard side. The gangway lay on the opposite side! We ran even harder, with me half dragged by Jay. The ship's crew were already pulling the gangway in.

"Wait!" yelled Jay, having removed his helmet as we rushed forward.

They stopped.

"Thanks," Jay and I gasped in unison, not stopping, continuing our awkward race down the gangway.

We jumped the last couple of mini steps. Up went the gangway immediately, the crew obviously as anxious to be rid of us as we did them. Then Jay was helping me take off the cumbersome helmet. I took great big, heaving gasps of air as the ship drifted fast away from the dock, pulled by the pilot-tug on the other side.

"You know, we didn't take you on board to sightsee," admonished Moodley, walking up to us.

Jay shook his head, wet with sweat, and gave a short laugh. "They are on board."

"What?"

"Malcolm and his psycho girlfriend."

I nodded confirmation, still too winded to speak.

"They attacked us by the hold entrance. We managed to lock them in there."

Moodley stared at us. "Are you telling me," he said slowly, "that you have two fugitives locked up in that ship's hold?"

Jay nodded just as slowly, holding Moodley's gaze.

We all turned to look at the dark bulk of *The Morning Star* swinging her bow, already picking up speed with having reached the entrance to the deeper channel between the sandbanks.

"You know," began Moodley almost in rumination. "It's a very tricky business re-docking a ship once she's reached that channel. Can't risk her stuck on the sandbanks."

Jay was nodding quietly in understanding and total agreement.

I stared at the two men open-mouthed. "But..!"

Jay spoke first. "It's not like they'll run out of air, or any-thing...How long before they get out of the harbour?"

"About fifteen to twenty minutes. Maybe forty minutes—at most. I'll notify the guys and Inspector Dube just now. They can have them off in about two, three hours."

The two men stood watching the toxin-carrying ship sail grace-fully off into the night.

"But..." I still couldn't believe Jay and Moodley were doing it. "That's too long! They might get sick!"

Jay had his secret smile again. "Serves them right." His voice was soft in the damp night air.

I watched with the two men as the ship drew further away, thinking about how many would have been ill or worse had Mal-colm and Sheila's plan succeeded. Not just for a few months but over a continuing period of time as toxic waste leached into the

Northwest's water-table. I thought about Lionel and Henry—their deaths—and of Sheila or Sheena, or whatever-her-name-was, saying that the water-table was not her problem. I thought, with a shiver, of Malcolm's cold smile and Sheila's smug one. Jay was right. They deserved this. It was no less than poetic justice. No lawyer could save them from the slow fate they'd have so callously inflicted on countless others they never would have met, nor have probably even regarded as human...

Jay hugged me close to his side. "It's all over. You're safe now."

I nodded my head against his chest, hugging him back. It *was* all finally over. I felt only incredible exhaustion.

Jay's breath was warm against my hair. "Shall I drive you to your parents?"

"What time is it?"

"About 10:30."

"It's a bit late."

I felt him nod. "You can stay the night on the *Drom*."

I nodded, yawning. I'd finally get to see his family's yacht.

* * *

Inspector Dube wasn't too pleased when he was finally told back at the Portnet building, but was pacified when he got to go along to make the arrests. He graciously agreed, at Jay's suggestion and seeing me sway with exhaustion, to take our statements the following morning. Jay gave him the yacht's berth and his contact numbers, then we left for the yacht basin.

In my numbing weariness, I stared almost mesmerised by the reflection of the lights on the dark water, hardly noticing much of *The Elegant Dromedary* as she was registered. Jay helped me over the rails, half-carrying me. After we'd briefly greeted his parents, he showed me the little WC and my bunk. It was in the bow, a narrow triangular space, but boasting a comfortable bunk.

"You'll be okay?"

I smiled back wanly. "Once I've slept for about a year."

He grinned back, then was gone.

His mother came over while I was still taking off my boots. I hadn't spoken to her in years.

She smiled with warmth. "Thought you might need some things." She handed me a toiletry bag and an oversized T-shirt that looked like it might have been one of Jay's.

I smiled back. "Thanks! I really appreciate it."

There was an awkward little silence.

"Would you like something to eat...or drink, perhaps?"

I shook my head, a slight headache developing. "No thanks. I'm fine."

She nodded with another smile and left. I began to remove my sweatshirt.

She was back with an apologetic smile and a bottle of water. "You'd best have this."

"Thanks!" At the sight of the bottle I realised just how thirsty I was, and opened it to take a welcome sip.

Jay's mother stood watching me, a strange concern and appraisal in her look, so like Jay's sometimes. I must have looked a bit uncomfortable and questioningly at her, because she suddenly smiled warmly and said, "Right. Goodnight then. If you need anything, just shout."

I nodded with a half-smile, swigging from the bottle, as she left pulling the little door behind her. I put on the T-shirt then crawled under the covers, expecting to sleep like a log.

I couldn't fall asleep.

The gentle rocking of the boat was soothing, but the lap of water against the hull and the play of light reflected on the walls created a strange underwater effect I found disconcerting. The creak of the mooring ropes brought me back to alertness every few seconds. Besides, my mind and emotions were in a whirl. A kaleidoscope of faces and half conversations drifted through my mind: Terry, Jay, Malcolm and Sheila. And Jay's mum. I frowned, puzzled. I'd only met her a few times before.

She'd always struck me as cool and vaguely disapproving, not friendly like now. Back then, she'd bring tall beauties to introduce to Jay at his parties, or whilst I was visiting, always all but ignoring me. To my discomfort and amusement, Jay would use me as a foil against them all. But people do change... Strange, now that I thought about it, how protective of her independent son his mother had always been whenever I was around. I thought, too, of what Patty had said: that Jay wanted to marry me. He'd never said so to me...But Magda had said the same. In fact, everyone seemed to treat us as a couple. And what had Jay been wanting to say just before Henry had walked into the Wimpy?

I tossed and turned restlessly.

Then there was Terry who, apparently, really wanted to marry me—for some reason. Terry who could be charming and sweet one minute, and terrifyingly violent and aggressive the next. Could I trust such a man? I remembered how he'd swung at Jay in the Portnet building, how he always assumed command, how he always worked on the assumption that he—and only he—was right. So at odds with Jay helping the police where-ever he could. The only person Jay refused to co-operate with, was Terry. And who could blame him? Jay had said Terry would stifle me, make me fit his life-style, and I'd thought then I'd be fine with that... But it was also all too easy to imagine Terry turning his violence and aggression on me. Was that a risk I could afford to take?

I kicked off the suffocating duvet.

Terry was exciting and handsome, every woman's dream. Terry had said he loved me, wanted to marry me, would take care of me and protect me...all the things I'd needed to hear. But he wasn't there for me like Jay was. *He could never be there for me like Jay could...*

I doubted anyone else could either. How rare was Jay's telepathic communication with me? One in a thousand? One in a hundred thousand? Or was it rarer: one in a million or billion?

Terry, I could see now, would always try to control things around him—and that would inevitably include me.

I fell asleep eventually, wondering how many things in my life and self I'd need to compromise to be Terry's wife and have a happy marriage with him.

* * *

I awoke bleary-eyed, feeling tense and exhausted.

Outside, the sun shone incredibly bright and wintry. Moving stiffly, I got up to totter to the WC. It felt strange to use it—so like an aeroplane's. Going back to my bunk, I pulled on my trousers then followed the soft lull of voices. The boat rolled to port-side just as I began to climb the stairs up to the deck, making me clutch the hatchway in alarm. Poking my head up with caution, I squinted into the sunlight.

"There you are!" greeted Jay's mum from behind her sunglasses, looking immaculate as usual. "Sleep well?"

"Erm, *ja*."

Her smiled was amused, recognising politeness when she heard it. "You've just missed Jay. He went off to scrounge for some break-fast. There's some coffee, if you'd like."

I grinned, conscious of the aroma. My favourite Kenyan blend, same as Jay's and, it seemed, his mother's. "Coffee would be great."

"Help yourself." She indicated a little percolator.

There were biscuits too: shortbread and chocolate brownies. I sat down across from her in the little seated area sunk into the deck, trying to be as ladylike as I could.

"You've had quite a bad time these past few weeks?"

"Yes. If it hadn't been for Jay..."

"Yes..."

We sat in companionable silence for a minute or two. She was studying me again, to my growing discomfort. I tried not to mind, concentrating on the familiar smell of coffee to calm me down.

"You know," she eventually confessed, "it was always very hard for me to accept Jay's fondness of you. I could never see what he saw in you—your potential. But I can see it now."

I stared at her in bewilderment, forgotten biscuit melting in my mouth, lips coated by crumbs. "I'm sorry," I mumbled, wiping my mouth. "I don't quite follow."

"Well, maybe potential is the wrong word. Heart, perhaps, is a better word. I believe now that you'll make an excellent mother. And you seem to be a wonderful influence on Jay. I can finally see why he loves you. And I do want more grandchildren! They're such a joy." She smiled.

"But, we're not..." I stammered. "Jay's not...He's not asked me to marry him," I blurted out.

"Oh, but he will," she assured me conspiratorially with a nod of her head. Then, "Would you look at the time!" She stood up. "I have breakfast with Janice. You'll be alright here. Jay won't be long." She bent over me, quite unexpectedly, to plant a soft, affectionate peck on my cheek, then left with a roll of the yacht.

I stared, stunned as I watched her walk gracefully along the dock, biscuit crumbs still on my mouth. I wiped them away absentmindedly, then cupped my still hot cup of coffee in both hands, luxuriating in the warmth of the liquid and the sunlight. I stretched my legs out to bask and thought of absolutely nothing.

* * *

Jay arrived soon after with a selection of pastries and Inspector Dube. They were both joking and laughing. The Inspector accepted a pastry and some coffee while he took our statements. It took longer than I expected. I liked the Inspector. For some reason, the word 'jolly' always came to mind every time I saw him. An old-fashioned, simple word to describe an old-fashioned, uncomplicated, kind person.

"We appreciate all you two have done," he was saying. "As well as all the information your Scottish friend sent us, Mr Duart."

I gazed at Jay in surprise. I hadn't realised he'd had Tom send information over to the police here.

"But, of course, we can't do more officially to thank you, as I'd like. So, all I can do is personally thank you on behalf of myself and my colleagues. I can't tell you how much we appreciate your help and co-operation, as well as the risks you took. It wouldn't have been such a good ending without you," this mostly to Jay.

Jay acknowledged with a nod of his head. "You'd have done the same." He wasn't just being polite and the Inspector knew it.

He flashed us both a broad smile, taking his leave, shaking our hands with both of his. "I wish to meet you two again under happier, less dangerous circumstances."

"Likewise," Jay answered for both of us.

The Inspector stepped off the boat, turning once to wave good-bye as he walked down the dock.

"Nice man," remarked Jay.

"*Ja*, I like him too."

"I called your mum and dad. They insisted on coming to fetch you."

"They would." And suddenly there seemed nothing else to be said, and yet so much to say...

We stood looking over the yachts rolling gently in the early morning breeze. I still felt exhausted, but in a good way, like the end of an interminable shift with impossible deadlines that you somehow meet anyway.

I looked at Jay. It was almost as if I was seeing him for the first time. The sunlight accentuated his long, dark eyelashes and made his eyes appear very light. His face had changed a little, the gaunt-ness of his youth replaced with a handsomeness. He looked mature, his expression more open and kind. At that moment, I realised he was the most beautiful man on earth.

"Don't look at me like that if you don't mean it," he said softly, still staring at the bobbing yachts.

I looked away regretfully. "It would never work anyway," I said.

He didn't look at me.

"You have your job in Norway and it would be difficult for me to move. Long distance relationships, especially trans-continental ones, are exceeding difficult... And you'll have to make your new home. You'll be extremely busy."

We stood together, the air still heavy with emotion. Seagulls dove onto the shore near the Yacht Club, fighting over something. Jay spoke first.

"I've always felt," his voice was gentle and wistful, "that home was where you were, Sammi."

I blinked, ambushed by unexpected tears. I tried to speak, but no sound came out my suddenly tight throat. I cleared my throat and tried again, sounding hoarse. "What are you saying? That you wouldn't go to Norway? Because of me?"

He looked down at his feet then at me. "I'll go where-ever you want to go...If you want me to."

"Are you asking me to marry you?" I had to be sure.

"Yes." He looked down then up again. "Do you need to think about it?"

I shook my head. "No, I already know my answer."

He looked away again, sighing tiredly. "You really like that Grierson, then?"

I shrugged. "He's okay...But it's you I love," I burst out.

Jay whipped around. "You do?"

"Yes, I want to marry you!"

He picked me up into a hug, laughing and smiling. And then he kissed me with sweetness and tenderness, and unspoken but binding promises.

A few minutes later, I hugged him close and tried to get my breath back.

"You choose where we live," said Jay generously.

I shook my head. "No. We both decide. Besides, I've been think-ing...A change would do me good. And I love that idea about that methane power-plant."

"Really?"

"Yes. It fits in well with my new perspective on environmental protection."

Jay laughed and kissed me again, hugging me closer. I peeked up at the safe world, at a fluffy cloud floating past his t-shirt sleeve. My wish had come true after all. I'd finally met my husband—an older, wiser, sweeter version of my best friend. And I smiled in true happiness I'd never known before.

#

Excerpt: Situation No Win

Tom and Liu thought they'd made the discovery of a lifetime when the ancient relic they're studying reveals amazing properties. Now, Liu's dead and Tom's on the run with few he can trust. Running into naive school teacher, Melissa, again could be Tom's salvation, or his ruin if he can't stop falling in love with her.

From the deserts of Shaanxi Province, China to the coast of South Africa, Tom and Melissa have to navigate history, dodge the unscrupulous and psychotic, and stay alive to rewrite their own stories. But with double-crosses and fiendish plans the order of the day, who will end up with naught?

<h1 style="text-align:center">Chapter One</h1>

Monkey King Vs Highlander

The Mu Desert, China, 2010

Tom avoided Liu's striking arm, leaned back against the make-shift lab counter and rolled out of range of his friend's enthusiasm.

"You die now, you filthy Scottish scum!" yelled Liu, really getting into the spirit of their mock fight, his cross-eyed squint lending him a comedic menace.

Tom suppressed a giggle. So, he hadn't showered in two days, well neither had Liu. Still, he couldn't let that insult pass. It was time to introduce something new to this fight.

He ducked under a free-standing table and grabbed his retractable practice sword lying next to bubble-wrapped ancient swords: recently unearthed; recently catalogued; and awaiting careful shipment to Xi'an.

Holding his sword with both hands and striking the immortal pose, Tom yelled back with a hundred percent Scottish burr, "There can be only one!" He stared with lower eyebrows at his best friend's maniacal grin. He knew what Liu was thinking; they'd argued about it for hours on end only just last week: Monkey King Vs Highlander, who'd win?

Liu put the relic he held into his jacket pocket, and dropped into a fighting stance. The puzzling cylinder, dug up less than a week ago still awaited full analysis of its strange chemical composition and enigmatic writing. Bulging at his side, it would have been safer with the bubble-wrapped swords but Liu refused to be parted from the artefact until he personally delivered it to Xi'an.

Tom grinned. He had the greater reach with his sword and longer arms, though they'd both need to be extra careful not to inadvertently damage the relic. Dr Zhou, Liu's uncle and the Excavation Director, would be heart-broken; it would be unprofessional; and quite possibly the end Liu's career and of Tom's stay in China...or worse.

If thoughts of similar disgrace were going through Liu's mind he didn't show it as he went through a precise martial arts movement while making Bruce Lee sounds.

Tom dampened his grin, admiring his friend's practised flowing Tai Chi movements, and moved into open space in the roomy tent. Liu moved parallel to him, a whirl of movement.

Tom spun around, feeling he was definitely losing the mock battle in some way, and brought the sword overhead, posing dramatically, his face a mock snarl.

Liu was momentarily surprised, then concentrated even more, anticipating his friend's charge.

Tom tensed, muscles set to launch towards Liu, brows furrowed for half a second. The air was electric, like a storm approaching, and was Liu's favourite relic starting to glow even through the material of his clothes?

Tom would have hesitated but was already committed to the charge. He swept forward, swinging his sword in an arc.

Liu slid down in a snake-like motion and brought his hand forward, brushing the relic at his side.

The air sparkled with electric dust, and a shocked Tom flew backwards, landing with a crash amongst packaging boxes and markers.

Liu's horrified brown eyes met Tom's appalled grey ones. With trembling hands, Liu withdrew the relic from his pocket. It *was* glowing! What else could it do? Both friends gazed at the octagonal coppery cylinder. The odd, unreadable inscriptions running its length offered no answers.

* * *

Tom hurried along the Shenmu street beside the river. Erlang-shan Temple rose like a castle on the ridge above him. Across the valley in which the little city sat sprawled the Nine Dragon Temple rock-faces and pagoda with the glittering golden Immortal overseeing all. A slight breeze made the humidity and strong sun just bearable, reminding Tom why the Mu Desert was one of his favourite places. He breathed in the clean air so unlike most larger cities and smiled at familiar faces as he'd smiled at his friend, Yan, at the temple.

The monk, knowledgeable than most about the region's history and oddities, hadn't heard of a relic with the powers Liu's strange cylinder held but it was early days in their research and the artefact would soon be in Xi'an. Besides, Tom had enjoyed the conversation with the amusing wise man, who promised to mention the relic to the abbot of HuiShan Monastery where many ancient manuscripts were in the process of being transcribed. Nevertheless, Tom was nervous talking about the relic to anyone, even Yan whom he trusted. He'd convinced Liu and Dr Zhou to remove the photo of the artefact from the camp's website and to keep news of it as low-key as possible until the relic was studied at the main lab in Xi'an. Gibson was already asking questions about the incident with Liu and the relic, and knowing his director as he did, that made Tom very nervous indeed. Exciting though the discovery was, Tom wished they hadn't found the intriguing artefact. He already missed the worry-free days when all they'd found were stone inscriptions and graffiti, remnants of old villages, and farm and construction technology.

Weaving past shoppers and groups of schoolkids making their way back to classes from lunch, Tom dove into the refreshing air-conditioning of the local KFC. Jimmy, one of the team from the dig, grinned and waved from a table by the window while talking into his phone. Mobile reception wasn't the best back at camp. Tom waved back then turned his attention to the server, glad the lunch-time rush was over. He hated waiting in line. The KFC was almost empty. Besides Jimmy, there were only two other patrons—a guy with mirrored wraparound glasses and an iPhone who got the once-over in return, and a student playing a game on their little phone.

Tom gave the menu a cursory glance, checking the seasonal fish and chicken combos were still available. Less than five minutes later, Tom, his body relaxing as he descended, took his tray downstairs to the dim, cool basement seating where Liu would be found,.

For a change, Liu wasn't alone. He was laughing, sitting across from a familiar-looking girl. Tom walked over, anxiety creeping over him. Should he know this girl with the unfashionable poor-boy hat? Surely he hadn't gone out with her in his early days in Shenmu. She wasn't his type, not in those faded loose jeans and shapeless shirt. Up close, she appeared older than he'd first thought, around his age—late thirties for sure.

"Ah, here he is!" said Liu in English, his eyes twinkling with mischief. "Our famous Tom MacKenzie, all the way from Scotland."

Tom slid his tray alongside Liu's, reluctant to initiate any contact with the woman. Let her think he was disinterested. It would be the truth.

She half-rose, awkward in the small space of the booth and held out a hand. "Hi! I'm Melissa. Liu's been telling me all about you."

Startled by her accent, Tom met her hazel eyes, and wished he hadn't. He looked away immediately, taking his seat and rumbled a greeting. She wasn't Chinese though she might have been Asian; her accent English, Canadian or Australian. And if she was in Shenmu, that could only mean she was an English teacher at one of the schools. She looked the type and Shenmu didn't attract many tourists—not yet. Tom continued analysing her, speculating so he wouldn't have to think about that shock of electricity he'd experienced when their eyes met. He stole a glance as she settled into her seat again. She appeared flustered. Had she felt it too?

The strained silence was broken by a frowning Liu. "So, I was just telling Melissa about our remarkable find."

Tom's head whipped towards his friend, a glower on his face.

"She's eager to see our website and very interested in our work," said Liu, turning to face both, with a smile for Melissa.

"*Ja!* I love archaeology and history!" said Melissa, picking up her tea. "I've been to a couple of the temples around here, and your camp sounds fascinating."

"No visitors allowed," stated Tom.

Melissa's cheerfulness turned into confusion. "I wasn't..."

Liu sighed. "Of course. Though she's welcome to follow our progress and learn more online. And I'd be honoured if you do, Melissa *Laoshi!*" His eyes and head flicked from Tom to her and back again: *Go on. Be nice!*

Tom tried not to roll his eyes. *Here we go again!* Just because he hadn't been on a date recently. Liu would have already taken her through the local custom of subjecting new acquaintances to painstaking, intensely personal questions: How old are you? Are you married? Where are your parents from? Where do you work? Why did you come to Shenmu and not stay in Xi'an...?

Liu kicked Tom's feet. "Melissa's a teacher in Yulin."

So, that's where he might have seen her, during their monthly big shop or on the train to Xi'an. Still, she seemed more familiar than simply a face at the station or the KFC. Tom risked looking at her again. She nodded.

"*Ja*, not as interesting as your jobs, but I love it. The kids here are great!"

Definitely, not his type, then.

"So, what exactly do you do, Tom? Are you also an archaeologist like Liu?" Her voice was politely formal.

She made eye contact and Tom's mind blanked for a second, that earlier anxiety reasserting itself along with confusion and, perhaps, disappointment. Did she prefer Liu? Not that he'd mind, but...

"Technical writer," said Tom, sounding gruff instead of matter-of-fact.

"Oh. That's nice. Unusual. I've never met a technical writer before." She turned her full, attention to Liu. "So, what's it like being an archaeologist? Do you do Indiana Jones stuff?"

Liu laughed and she laughed with him, looking cute and carefree, with no hint of the stern-face she'd given Tom, though to be honest he might have deserved it for being such a rude *eejit*.

Tom stare at Melissa was intense, stewing in wordless emotion. Why did he feel he was at an interview and losing the job? The sense he'd known her before niggled more than ever. And why was he feeling so confused? He didn't even like her! She wasn't his type. All he knew was he didn't want her going out with Liu either—or with anyone else. Tom was shocked at himself. *This couldn't be love at first sight, could it? That was only a fable. And not with her—a mousey, unfashionable English teacher! This jealousy he was feeling was simply his sense of competition with Liu, 'cos Tom MacKenzie didn't do love. Not any more.*

Looking for a distraction as he chewed on crumbed fish-sticks, Tom watched Jimmy descend the stairs. Lingering on the third from last step, the interpreter scanned the empty basement as if searching for a friend. His gaze drifted to Liu and Melissa, then met Tom's eye. He smiled almost bashfully, and climbed up the stairs again. Tom watched Jimmy, unsettled. His hunches were strong—a gift from a long line of infamous witchy ancestors—a gift he'd been grateful for more than once. The hunch he had now told him something, other than the fish-stick, was fishy. Did Jimmy know Melissa? And if he did, what did that mean? How much had Liu told her about the relic? Tom shivered. The less people who knew about that odd device and its powers, the better. He'd have a word with Liu about the security on the drive back to camp when they'd be assured a modicum of privacy.

* * *

Half an hour later, Melissa made her goodbyes on the wide street outside the KFC, saying she hoped to get the fast bus back to Yulin. Liu exchanged email addresses with her while Tom stood in moody silence growing more surly. They both watched her walk towards the bus station, turning once to wave. She turned down a side alley and narrowly avoided being run over by a motorbike taxi swerving away from one of the many black Range Rovers with tinted windows driving in the city.

In their own white Landcruiser, Tom waited until Liu had navigated out of the valley and they were crawling up towards the highway on the steep road made narrower by construction. "We have to find a way to keep that device safer. Keep it quiet 'til we know who we can trust with it."

"I agree," said Liu.

"So why tell Melissa about it?"

Liu smiled and glanced at him. "You're not the only one with 'hunches' and gut-feelings, my friend. I think that nice lady will be significant in our lives."

"How? She's an English teacher! To little kiddies."

Liu grinned. "A well-loved one, I'm told. She can help educate those kiddies about the importance of history, archaeology, preserving—"

"You really like her, don't you?" Tom watched the endless line of barely moving coal-trucks that would only end once they reached the highway. It wasn't that he was jealous...just concerned for his friend.

Liu, having thought about it, took a well-calculated opportunity to dodge around a slow-moving tri-wheeled car, then asked, "Don't you?"

Tom wasn't going down that route. "We know nothing about her. How can you trust her?"

Liu half-shrugged, hanging onto the wheel as the road edged closer to the cliff dropping all the way down to the valley littered with planted conifers and sparse scrubs. "I have a feeling—a very good feeling—that Melissa will be a good friend and is totally trustworthy, the kind my ancestors would approve of just as they approve of you, Tom Mackenzie." He shot a grin at the Scotsman.

A suicidal biker zoomed up to past them in the negligible space between the trucks and the Landcruiser. Liu swerved in reflex towards the cliff. Tom's heart leapt in his throat as the Landcruiser wheels on his side skimmed the cliff edge. Liu swore and corrected their path, taking them back to relative safety. They glanced at each other, then laughed in relief.

"Too close," said Liu.

"Yeah, you had me hanging there for a second," shot back Tom. He continued bantering with his friend, hiding his growing sense of foreboding.

A large black Range Rover pulled up behind them, perhaps the same one he'd spotted in Shenmu. The back of his neck prickled. He hated to think what would happen if its driver decided to copy the biker's behaviour. Fortunately, they were almost to the highway and the road was widening as they neared the on-ramps. He needed to discuss more security measures with Liu. His paranoia was returning, but it was more important than ever to take extra measures after that close call. Nobody knew about the relic as much as Liu and him, and he wasn't going to chance that kind of power falling into the wrong hands.

Tom allowed himself to relax again only after the black SUV took another on-ramp and theirs was the only vehicle heading off towards the ancient dunes.

* * *

Two weeks later, Liu tapped a nervous tattoo against the table with his mini-trowel, sweat forming rivulets down his back. His tent was not the most comfortable place in this unseasonably hot desert night, the unusual mugginess making the heat even more unbearable. He dared not venture outside into the cooler night to find a relieving breeze on a high dune. They'd surely get him then.

He peered at his watch in exasperation. Where was Tom? He was only meant to be documenting the new finds in Camp Two, not the whole excavation!

Liu turned off the lamp. Standing at the tent flap, he peered out with great caution. Should he risk going to his Uncle Zhou? Liu considered for a few breaths. His uncle was a gentle scholar, oblivious to most evils. He'd be no help in the present circumstances. They'd kill his uncle much more easily than they'd kill him—of that Liu was certain. No, the only person he could trust was Tom.

And Tom was still out there running hours late.

Liu shivered. Had they gotten Tom already? Had they made Tom show them where the device lay hidden? Liu took a step back. Surely not. Tom was too careful and could handle trouble.

Liu fretted, still looking at the tent flap. Tom had better get here soon! He desperately needed to tell his friend about the new discovery he'd made.

Liu fingered the small object in his pocket. The now familiar growing tingle it produced was a small comfort. He couldn't risk keeping more of the device intact. Extracting this key component had been easy and necessary. Besides, it was simpler to conceal.

The air was suffocating. Outside, the wind was picking up again, blowing in from the west. Dust storms wouldn't be far behind. That would slow Tom's team down.

Decision made, and with a growing sense of despair, Liu worked quickly.

Taking his broken, but still in use, retractable Tai Chi practice sword, Liu tried to force the small stone from his pocket into the hole left by the missing piece. It wouldn't fit.

Sweating even more, he wrestled another segment out. The stone fitted this time, wedging securely against the edges. Satisfied, Liu capped the metal ends of the sword with its plastic cover and laid it gently down amidst his notes; a newly scrawled one in that binary code looking remarkably like a doodle. A derisive Tom had once shown him that trick. It would catch his friend's eye.

Next, Liu burnt his schematics of the ancient device and all his personal notes on it. He scattered the ashes on the sand floor at the entrance to the tent. All he could do now was wait for the men he was sure were coming for him that night.

He waited for over an hour.

The adrenalin rush that had kept him alert earlier was all but gone. Barely a few hours earlier, it had saved him from being trapped in the pit with those two men staring down. All those years at school playing The Monkey King in *Journey To the West* had been of use after all. He prayed to GuanYin and hoped she'd remember him after all these years. He hadn't prayed to her since back in high school...

A confused bug hit the tent; the distinct sound jerking Liu awake. He hadn't realised he'd fallen asleep. The wind had picked up even more. The storm had arrived. Liu tensed, straining to hear above the sand-blasted canvas. Not much else could be discerned but they were out there. He knew it; could feel it. He crept softly to his bunk and lay down.

They might not be aware he was expecting them. He still had a chance of surviving the night, if only a slim one. He had much to live for, especially now that the safety of the ancient device depended on him and Tom alone. Liu resolved to do all in his power to stop it falling into the hands of people who'd use it for evil. It was the only thing to be done. And if he was to die here, he'd not die in vain. Through half-closed eyes, Liu watched the tent flap slide slowly aside allowing some dust and two men to creep in. Liu clutched his trowel tightly. It was time to live or die.

* * *

Tom hit the sand with a groan, his chest almost paralysed by the cruel blow. He barely managed to roll away from the swinging boot. It jarred his shoulder and sent him tumbling down the dune.

His two attackers followed his descent. They didn't know Liu had dismantled part of the relic. Neither could they know he'd hidden those parts in the cave. He could never risk telling them; they'd kill him anyway, just as they'd said they'd done to Liu.

At the bottom of the dune, Tom pushed to his feet and began a staggering run into the approaching storm. He had to get help. Even if he couldn't make it back to camp, he had to keep the relic safe if it was the last thing he ever did.

Panting with effort and spitting sand blasted up by the rising wind, one question raced through Tom's mind: Who had sent these murderers?

End of excerpt.

Ask for Situation No Win *at your favourite independent book store or request it from your local library. Also available as an eBook and through digital library services.*

ABOUT LEENNA

Leenna writes cross-genre suspense, romance, and dabbles in sci-fi/fantasy. She also reads the tarot. Her short stories have appeared in *Mad Scientist Journal, SciPhi Journal,* and *Cosmic Roots And Eldritch Shores* where she also serves as editor to the Myths, Legends and Fairy Tales department. When not writing, she often tries her hand at anything vaguely artistic.

Leenna's most unnerving experiences include: looking a red kangaroo in the eye, flipping pancakes for the first time ever in front of her class, interviewing Alan Dean Foster (even though it was via email), and teaching a hellhound how to share a biscuit. Sometimes she writes about these and other less nerve-wracking things; sometimes she doesn't.

Find Leenna at:

https://leennanaidoo.wordpress.com
https://leennascreativebox.com
https://www.patreon.com/LeennaNaidoo **(free eBooks for patrons!)**

What's in the juice?

Angie accompanies her engineer husband to Mars to spend more quality time together. But with Kieron working hard, she's got more than enough time to wonder at the strange changes and caginess of the locals. Does the unverified report of an ET visit have anything to do with it? Angie becomes certain there's something in the juice the locals won't share, but what could it possibly be?

From mad scientists to familiar aliens, to Irish gods who only make Halloween dates, and the odd dragon making an unexpected appearance, they're all here in this collection of micro-, flash- and short-fiction.
Meet the shape-shifters and the scientists who just may be able take some tails too far. There's the depressed love-lorn lady who meets a surfer-dude of note, and the cookbook writer hosting the Dark Man of Erskine. Have a beer with the geologist who knows their unalienable right, while you try to spot Medusa, if you can. And if it's all too much, let the ELFs save you, or find your most cost-effective way to Mars.

Sighting: Possible Canid. Likely a werewolf
Location: Walpole, Western Australia
Status: Developing—tracking and research

When Stacy hires a cabin at in the quiet Walpole forest, the last creature she expects to meet is a wolf. Now he's got evil designs on her, but he hasn't counted on the locals' personal interest in matters.

Shy forester, Ash, just wants to meet the beautiful new visitor in the forest cabin and research that strange spoor he's spotted. Events take a dangerous turn when the tracks turn out to be a werewolf's, and the visitor a crypto-zoologist. Ash will have to think fast to keep the peace in his beloved forest and win his lady love. (*short story*)

OTHER BOOKS BY LEENNA

Fiction

I Find Myself Charmed
Three Million's A Crowd
Unsettled
Settle Down Now
Surviving Oblivion
Ride The Wave, Kiss The God
Dear Santa
Foreigners
The Bagua and Other Stories

Non-Fiction

How Not To Meet The Man Of Your Dreams
Your Tarotscopes 2017
Your Tarotscopes 2018

www.ingramcontent.com/pod-product-compliance
Lightning Source LLC
Chambersburg PA
CBHW032023050726
47590CB00006B/2285